Appetite For **Blood**

By

Amber
Anthony

ISBN 978-0-578-41837-7

Credits
Cover Artist: Kelly Martin
Editor: Dennis Hays
Printed in the United States of America
July 5, 2021

Praise for The Blood Trilogy

Blood Rising
"Sexy hot vamps, a dark secret and a fatal attraction.
What more can you want? Well written and a captivating
story, leaves you wanting more."
– J.K.R., Amazon, UK

Blood Emerald
"What a divine adventure awaits the reader inside
the five-hundred-year-old realm of the Hiatt empire.
Looking forward to reading the sequel, Blood Dragon!"
-    A.M.D., Goodreads, USA

Blood Dragon
"A Shifter romance to curl up with and enjoy, five stars!"
-    M.S., Goodreads, USA

"They shouldn't be together for so many reasons,
But, man, do they belong together!"
-    H.M., Amazon, USA

"I will definitely be reading this series again and again."
-    K.T., Amazon, USA

Praise for Becoming Gabriel

Gabriel is the perfect combination of masculinity, hero, and gentle angel. The story was beautifully orchestrated from start to finish. Oh, and did I mention the love scenes...yes please! This is such a unique tale. I could go on endlessly praising Amber Anthony's latest release. Oh, and by the way, Becoming Gabriel would make a fabulous movie. This five-star read has me waiting for their future works with bated breath!
-    A.M.D., USA

This book is great departure from Amber's paranormal romances. Gabe is Baltimore bred and could end up Baltimore dead if he doesn't fly right. Do his good looks get in the way of living right?... I was swept away within their drama. A love story for the city.
-    L.R., USA

Gabriel and Grace are a swoon-worthy romantic couple. Wow! I fell in love with him right along with Grace! When hard knocks hit, I agonized! I couldn't put this book down! What a riveting and well-written story! I will search for more work by Amber Anthony. I haven't enjoyed a read this much in months!
-J.P., USA

A five-star Great romantic suspense!
A.C., USA

Personal Credits

To Tim Bader, Rusty's husband, who supports us with lots of good humor and loving patience.

To Dorothy Fontana, who taught us to focus on the story, to put our characters up a tree and throw rocks at them.

To Dennis Hays, the verbal blacksmith, for guiding us in refining and clarifying prose.

To Kelly A. Martin, for translating our characters into evocative images.

To Jan Janssen, for her encouragement.

With their help, we step bravely into independent publishing. Thank you from both halves of Amber Anthony.

Dedication to our Readers

This origins novella is dedicated to the saving power of friendship. To readers and friends who wondered how Matthew Brenner, Richard Hiatt and Adam Lachlan came together.

It started this way…

Prologue

Los Angeles in the 1920s was a spectacular metropolis. The name Hollywood became synonymous with the United States film industry. The nation developed an appetite for moving pictures entertainment.

The aftermath of World War I brought damaged souls, too beautiful to work a trade, into the City of Angels to seek their fortune in 'movies'. Speakeasies flourished. Los Angelinos had an appetite for excitement.

Hollywood Boulevard was the main thoroughfare of the Hollywood district of Los Angeles. Sunset Boulevard added to the glamorous age of Hollywood from the 1920s through today. City residents gained an appetite for brushes with fame.

The area's growing undead population discretely culled the underbelly of the city to survive. But a new age was dawning. One enterprising vampire saw opportunity using innocuous means to satisfy their undead hunger. But their sole appetite? *The appetite for blood.*

1

"Dateline, August 1, 1922. Listen to this!" Matt Brenner, perennially twenty-eight years old, startlingly handsome and a fledgling vampire, snapped open the Los Angeles Times newspaper. "They hid the report in the back of the A section. It's not even with the crime beat."

Rick Hiatt, astute businessman, philanthropist, and vampire of four hundred years, glanced up briefly from his Wall Street Journal. "What is it, dear boy? You still looking for your death notice?"

"You slay me." Matt lowered the paper to glower, but Rick was back into the stock listings. "So, listen, they found another dead body within a mile or so of Veronique Moreau's joint."

"Why do you suspect vamps from her joint are to blame?"

"Coroner has ruled it suicide."

Rick raised an eyebrow and lowered the paper. "And?"

"And… 'The corpse was found *drained of blood*. The Los Angeles Homicide Squad postulated the victim, Sue Ellen Graves from Dubuque, Iowa, committed suicide by severing a large vein in her neck. "There was no blood found near the body," Detective Ballard states, "she was probably found and dumped by an acquaintance." Miss Graves came to Los Angeles after winning a screen test competition for Monarch Productions'."

"Ah, yes, Monarch Productions, owned by Francois Moreau, Veronique's infamous Papa."

"I'll bet the shields in homicide have a baker's dozen of unsolved murders in that area." Matt flicked the newspaper with his fingers. "I'd have been one of them if you hadn't been there."

"Matt, as satisfying as it would be to call the coppers about the Moreaus, you have to remember, you'd be sending mortals up against vampires. This is not their business."

"Whose business is it? Do responsible vampires tag-team rescuing people like me?"

"You were fortunate I happened by. Most vamps would never interfere with the Moreaus."

"So, they run amok, killing innocents?"

Rick shrugged an elegant shoulder. "They kill to feed."

****

Seven Days Later

The Sunset Grande's art deco elegance usually came alive at twilight. Not tonight. The animated din of flappers fueled by bathtub gin was silent. The building now only resonated the shuffling sound of moving men. Crews

4

bumped into the trompe l'oeil walls as they carted newsprint wrapped antiques down five flights of wide marble stairs. All the vamps who called the multi-story apartment building home wisely and discretely sought safer ground far from the magnifying glass of the authorities.

Rick, hands deep in his pleated trouser pockets, strolled around the fashionable setting with a calculating gaze. If Matt, his most recent rescue, and reluctant fledgling, was earnest in his desire to sell the place, Rick was determined he make the best profit possible off his unsought windfall.

The white linen of Rick's double-breasted business suit was impeccable. He pulled at the knot in his blue and lavender tie and cast an assessing look at Matt, who seemed even grimmer than usual if that was possible.

If Rick was the poster-boy bon-vivant, Matt was the moody adolescent by contrast. Both impossibly handsome in their own ways, light versus dark, snarky versus moody, all female fantasies were met between the two of them.

"Mr. Brenner, this property appraised for one and a quarter times your asking price. With a little patience, you could realize a greater profit."

"I don't care." Matt fisted his hands at his side, looking to Rick the perfect picture of contrary vampire immaturity.

The realtor aimed an imploring gaze at Rick, who shrugged. "It's Mr. Brenner's property."

"Very well, if you'll excuse me for a moment…" The man stepped into the double doorway and turned his back on Rick and Matt, to consult his notes.

Rick eyed his ward with irritation. "If you're determined to give away your money, why not make it a home for unwed mothers? I'll wager they don't live in this much marble and mahogany."

"I'm not giving it away. It's more money than I've ever made in my life. I have no desire to hold out for more. I want this finished."

"It's not like divesting yourself of this building will change your undead nature. Veronique turned you here. Yes, it was a rape turn, unwanted, unfair. You think you're behind the eight ball. But sell this building for the appraised price and you'll be in glad rags until the fifties." Matt gave him a scowl. "Remember, the undead live for centuries. You have to play the long game, now."

Matt turned to assess the ballroom, still heady with the scents of blood and sex. The stale air hung heavy, stagnant from the night, two weeks ago, when he was turned. Within ten days the Vampire Court pushed through a seal on Veronique's 'playhouse'. Influential vampires within the banking system froze her accounts and presented an impressive balance sheet to her victim, Matt.

The vampire crime princess borrowed enough money and influence from her family to escape within hours of her sentencing, but her family syndicate suffered significant losses. The apartment building housed one of Los Angeles' most fruitful speakeasies serving mortals and vamps alike. Public women with the goods to sell plied their trade in elegant studios. The exchange of bodily fluids went far beyond sex. And the sex itself surpassed any images from a bawdy stereoscope.

****

Matt glanced disdainfully across the opulent ballroom floor with its fanned mosaic marble pattern.

Is that dried blood in the crevices?

Every item in the room moaned debauchery. With a supernatural rush, he was in the realtor's face. Taken aback, the squat man gulped and nervously pushed his spectacles back up his nose.

"Sell it. Sell it for appraised value and don't bother me until you have a check."

"Yes, Mr. Brenner, as you…" The middle-aged man broke off in astonishment when two more gentlemen appeared beside him as if by magic.

"I may have an offer you'll wish to expedite." The taller and older of the two café-au-lait men began. His Haitian patois hinted at his close relationship to Veronique Moreau.

After an assessing beat, Matt's brows knitted. "You are…"

Rick was suddenly beside them, earning another gasp from the now totally confused realtor. "I don't believe you've met Jonas and Samuel Moreau, Veronique's brothers. Gentlemen." Matt noticed Rick did not extend a hand in greeting. "Meet your sister's latest illicit addition to the family."

A low growl emitted from Matt's throat and was answered by the two visitors, causing the agent to step back, turn and run, hat in hand.

Jonas, with a deep-tanned complexion and piercing blue-grey eyes, leveled a gaze at Matt as sharp as his cheekbones. He bowed stiffly, barely creasing his fine French tailored suit.

7

"What do you want?" Matt was in no mood for civility games.

Samuel, darker than his brother, with penetrating ebony eyes, was obviously in a similar mood. "We've come to make a reputable offer in good faith. You don't want this building, and we do."

Matt's hands unclenched, and his arms folded over the broad lapels of his pinch-back suit. "Yeah? What's in it for you?"

"We have a certain clientele we wish to continue serving."

"Really? I find your clientele bloodthirsty."

Jonas shrugged. "How are you, when you're hungry?"

Matt locked his jaw. "Not like them, and I'll burn this hellhole to the ground before I let you have it back."

Samuel waved a hand at Jonas. "This is pointless." He turned to Matt. "When you look back on the consequences, know we were prepared to make you a generous offer. What happens now is on your head."

Rick stepped between Matt and the interlopers. "You come into my city and spout off? No figures, just threats?"

Jonas tsked and chuckled. "Sell to us or your city burns."

"It may work that way in Haiti, gents, but this is sunny L.A. We have laws to protect our citizens, as your sister discovered. I'd hit the road if I were you before you find your shoulders minus your heads."

It could have been a car backfire, or a small explosion, or a gunshot. Matt was distracted enough to turn and by the time he turned back, the dangerous duo was gone. "What..." Rick sighed. "Typical of our Haitian friends, they bring the drama and disappear."

2

Matt Brenner disrobed and headed for his cool morning shower before going to ground. Even subterranean, he could feel the circadian pull of sunrise. As a fledgling vampire, it pained him to surrender to sunlight. Gone were the days of twenty-four-hour manhunts. Who would have imagined vampires of his age were more restricted than mortal teenagers? It was like having an adolescent curfew with the universe's burning discipline.

He soaped his muscled body and stared at the pattern in the Murano mosaic shower walls as his mind wandered to the places he could not go. The war seemed like yesterday. He'd been mustered out of the United States Army in June of 1919 with honors for his work as a spy. He served as a liaison with the group known as La Dame Blanche. This group was an intelligence network created in Belgium in 1916. His deep embedment consisted of observing and reporting enemy activities on the French railway. It was treacherous work. By the end of the war, he was one of a thousand agents covering the occupied territories.

Matt, who had a knack for languages, rose in the ranks until he served at the most dangerous post in Paris. The work resulted in little sleep and constant tension broken by stretches of utter boredom. Because he played the role of a brain-damaged young man, he was viewed as exempt from military service. He inhabited the character so well the Germans never questioned why he wasn't in uniform. Unfortunately, the role demanded he was constantly dirty, dressed in rags and, like most Parisians, half-starved.

Only the family who housed him for the Resistance knew he was not the wretch he appeared. He arrived in the summer and kept mostly to himself and the seclusion of the roof which had an unobstructed view of the train station. Matt quickly became friends with his hosts, Madame and Monsieur Simond. Their son was his age and had been lost fighting in the north. It was easy to think of them as parents, his role demanded it, and they welcomed him to the neighborhood as their disabled, distant cousin whose parents had been killed. Joining them for meals and sleeping on the roof was the only normalcy he eked out of his enlistment. For him, Paris was hardly 'wine, women and song'.

Within his Paris of crumbled stone and brick and the grey grit of debris, there was an oasis, the Simond's daughter, Anais. She skirted past him with soft, shy laughter whenever they found themselves alone together. Matt was definitely captivated by her petite and delicate beauty. She kept hens on the roof and between a few fat hens were some hidden homing pigeons. Matt killed time watching her cheerful, glowing face as she sang to her flock while he recorded troop movements and relayed news via the pigeons. Inevitably, their hands touched as he clamped messages onto the birds. Matt felt a stirring toward her, but she was so skittish he was hesitant to engage her, and he was concerned she was too young. Her slight figure made it difficult to guess her age and he could hardly ask Madam Simond.

When fall blew the first chill wind, Matt spent the day moping as his character would, searching through bombed out buildings 'liberating' scraps of wood. He dropped his bundle on the hearth of the sixth-floor walkup and yelped like a pinched puppy. This was the first time the demur Anais spoke to him directly.

"Oh, be careful! The wood is so dry, it splinters easily."

Matt stood shaking his splinter-gouged hand. "It's okay, I didn't hurt the wood."

Anais gazed at him through her eyelashes. "Silly man, I'm not concerned for the wood. You must remove the splinter, or it will fester."

Matt squinted in the semi-dark room and pinched at the palm of his hand. "Yeah, my mom always took way too much pleasure in digging out splinters. I'll try to suck it out."

She hurried toward him, catching his hands. "Non, your mouth is dirty. Stop! I have the perfect thing."

He stood smiling at the sound of her light footsteps running from room to room yelling to her family, "Where is my embroidery case?" She returned brandishing a pair of small sewing scissors. Matt backed into the corner. "Are you a bebe? I don't intend to hurt you. You won't even know I've done it."

They stood in the window's light as she clipped the wood from his palm in one smooth motion. Matt's eyes stayed closed long after she reassembled her case and ripped a small strip of muslin from her slip.

She wrapped his palm and giggled. "You can open your eyes, you're not even bleeding." When their gazes met, she blushed deeply and kissed the palm of his hand. "You're all better."

Matt winked. "Should I call you Androcles?"

Anais shook her head. "You are no lion…" She drew her hand up to cover her mouth and her bright blue gaze flashed bashfully up to his. "You are an Adonis."

Matt looked aside and bit his bottom lip. "Is my French so bad you think I'm stupid?" He cracked a grin that made her giggle. "People only raved about Adonis's looks, not his brain." She laughed wryly. Matt stepped back to check her expression. With a gentle hand, he swept her glossy, brown hair out of her eyes. "I'm right, aren't I? You think I'm stupid."

"I think you're charming and you play stupid well." She chuckled. "We have an unused tea bag; won't you join me for tea?"

Matt nodded soberly. "I'd love that." He sat at the table as she busied herself with the teapot. "Anais, I never see you with books, do you go to school?" She shook her head and his heart fluttered with optimism.

"I have completed my first year at the Sorbonne, but Papa decided I should stay home until the war is over."

"And… you're about 19?"

"Oui."

"I don't see any suitors calling on you?"

She rolled her eyes at him. "There is a war; any man I'd want is either dead or at the front."

"Any man?" Matt asked hopefully.

****

Every time he saw a pigeon take wing, he thought of Anais, and their sweet stolen moments spent on his pallet in the corner of the roof.

The following July, on a sultry night, in her modest way, she cuddled into his arms and whispered. "Do you really want to take me back to California?"

Matt breathed in her delightful violet scent. "If your parents would miss you, they can come too. Los Angeles needs an authentic boulangerie."

Her bright blue eyes contrasted with her creamy, soft complexion. She hid behind a wave of milk chocolate brown hair. He raised her chin to gaze into her sparkling eyes. "We'll make beautiful babies and they'll be French-American babies." She moved away from his romantic gaze. He paused. "Did I say the wrong thing?" Anais slid off his lap and folded her knees under her chin. Her arms wrapped around her legs.

"We may already have a French-American baby." Her cheeks colored, and she bit her bottom lip.

Matt rose and pulled her into a spin. He caught her precious face in both hands and kissed her nose. "Does that mean what I think it means?

She nodded with a hesitant smile. "You're going to be a papa in about six months."

He pulled back and looked at her closely. "That's what's different about you. That glow. I always thought the glow of expecting mothers was a myth. But you've got it." She ducked her head shyly. "Oh, we've got to get you and your family out of Paris right now. It's too dangerous here and you need to eat regularly."

"I want to stay with you. I want to be with you for this." She gently caught his hand and drew his palm to her belly. Their gazes caught fire as he felt the evidence of his child within her.

Matt felt faint. "Nan, I want you to be here too, but with a baby, no. You're not having my baby in the middle of a war."

"It is impossible to leave Paris now."

"I know someone. He can get you and your parents to Switzerland through Lake Geneva. I can't go with you, but you'll have them, and you and our little one will be safe." Matt searched the inky night sky. "We need to visit your priest…"

****

"With this ring, I thee wed, with my body, I thee worship, and with all my worldly goods, I do thee endow." Matt slid the ring made from woven, copper wire he stripped from an abandoned building, onto her finger. With the priest's permission, they kissed and accepted her parent's congratulations.

****

The horse-drawn wagon concealing citizens fleeing Paris would arrive in five days. Matt emphasized to Anais

14

and her family they must continue in all their daily rituals as if nothing unusual was at hand.

On the fourth day of their marriage, Matt returned to the simple home on Rue Du Cydne to find the building decimated by German tanks. The memory was still raw and one of those experiences of war men didn't talk about. Wandering through the ruins only confirmed his worst fear. Anais and her family lay like broken dolls among the scattered bricks. The pigeons returned, scratching, and cooing a requiem.

I'll see you again, one day, my beautiful Anais.

A sly-eyed woman with a crudely shaved head stood across the rubbled street. She pointed an accusing finger at him. "You, boy, you're not the half-wit you pretend. Why would Anais marry an idiot? Who are you?"

Matt's words exploded from his lips. "I know who you are by your shaved head, traitor!"

She ducked her head and covered the thin patches of hair with both hands. "Spy!" She pointed a bony finger at Matt. "Spy! Spy! Spy!" Her shrill accusation drew every available citizen from blocks around.

Matt scrambled over the piles of bricks in the street, intent on murder. The priest who married them grabbed the back of his jacket. "She is dammed, she'll die of disease, let her be. I need to get you out of here."

Matt stumbled, blinded by tears. "I need to bury my wife."

"Your wife and her family are bait. The Huns are watching for you. Come, noble young man, the church will see to them. I swear on my life."

Matt pulled out of the priest's grasp and slapped his chest with both hands. "Come and take me, I'm dead already." The priest hooked his arm around Matt's neck and dragged him into the shadows.

****

Far from his fantasy of taking on the entire German Army, Matt found himself isolated in a bell tower in the Couvent des Feuillants. Dressing as a nun didn't irritate him as much as shaving three times a day. He tried to tell himself he was doing it for home and country. And he secretly wondered if Anais guided his gaze the day, he spotted the German High Command skulking out of the last grand home standing at the end of the block. It wasn't enough, it wasn't nearly enough, but the sight of the once grand mansion raised to the ground with at least twenty of the highest-ranking German officers dead within its walls was some small solace.

Carrier pigeons, the most ordinary of birds, proved to be the destruction of the Paris occupation. They'd also paved Matt's path to freedom. But, today, he could not see birds without being thrown back into the painful memory and mourning his loss. It was one of the consolations of being undead that he saw few birds now, only awakening after sunset and going to ground before it rose.

Returning to post-war, sunny Los Angeles, his parents gave him a hero's welcome, unaware of his personal tragedy. He silently wore Anais's copper ring which the priest returned to him. It danced on a chain next to his heart.

He accepted the expectation that he'd find a job and be on his own in thirty days. The Los Angeles Police Department welcomed him to the Crime Crusher Division without requiring time as a flat foot. Once again, he was a rising star among detectives, working undercover until his good looks became too well known. Once that happened, he supervised the less conspicuous to nail organized crime in the city.

He moved into the largest distinctive bungalow his salary could support and accrued a selection of loud neckties and classic suits. At first, Matt spent his spare time alone on the beach, painting sunrises and sunsets. Now and then, his palette of oils attracted a curious bathing beauty.

After some months, he began to return conversations with the women who swamped him with flirty compliments. Anais was dead, his child was never born, and he was a single man. He stowed Anais's copper ring in his valet box. It was time to live again.

If he played his cards right, one of those flirtatious blonde beauties from the beach would accompany him to his art studio in the back of the bungalow. A little Victrola music, a little 'innocent' lemonade and a little moonlight might see her modeling in the altogether. If his romancing worked, he would escalate to a booth at Musso and Frank's and further. He really relished 'further'.

He was a popular guy. As he lay on his marble catafalque, he revisited memories of his abbreviated mortal adulthood.

Damn! I went from kid to soldier to cop to a vampire. I never got a life with the woman I loved. I never held my child and now, even in the afterlife, I am damned, and I never will. I wish Veronique had simply drained and discarded me.

Instead, he'd been thrust into the rarified atmosphere of swift vampire justice and extravagant living. His father worked a lifetime, and their family never had a tenth of the splendor he lived in now. With one macabre roll of the dice, he was immersed in bespoke suits and the finest luxuries, but he was the eternally damned, undead.

Rick rescued him, but just how long would it be before Matt was shown the door?

Where does a fledgling vampire find a home? Do I go back to my bungalow and become the odd bachelor who only comes out at night?

He sighed deeply. It wasn't a question he could answer today. He had enough faith in Rick to believe he would be given guidance before it was time for him to pack up. Whether vampire or mortal, he guessed life was full of uncertainties.

3

The exclusive Tiki Club, owned by Rick, welcomed every sheik and sheba on Wilshire Boulevard who had an *in*. If their appetite was for fine dining and dancing to the fluid tunes of Marisol and the Hector Lopez orchestra, the supper club was the place. If illegal, high octane beverages were desired, one cut through the small forest of live palm trees in the corner and wended their way down a narrow brick corridor to ascend a spiral staircase. Give the right knock and it was 'bottoms up'.

Rick enjoyed the 'cabbage', of course, a guy had to make a living. But the real thrill was all those beating hearts knocking down the doors for endless nights of entertainment. He acquired some of his most willing donors in exchange for entrée into the supper club. Word spread, and before long, the orgasmic thrill of donating to a vampire became legendary in the L.A. party world. Rick occasionally worried club rumors would rip away the fragile veil between mortal and undead. The Tiki Club mortals decided to trust the speakeasy's undead for sexual satisfaction in exchange for blood. The Moreaus continued to victimize mortals to feed, creating a glaring contrast between the two philosophies. Rick saw no reason, in the modern age, for vampires to kill to eat. He would rather thrill to eat.

If the few dozen vampires in Los Angeles needed a few hundred donors, imagine what the city would need in five years.

Gotta play the long game.

****

Rick pulled the Duesenberg up to the club's portico entrance. He climbed out, tossing the keys to his valet and Matt joined him seconds later. It was just past eight in the evening, and the blue nose dinner crowd began to arrive. The delicate darlings of society came out, dined, danced, and made it home by curfew. A few of the enlightened made it upstairs and the pleasures awaiting them flew them to the moon.

Even the sullen Matt couldn't seem to resist the gay atmosphere of conviviality. His smile, when he remembered it, was seductively devastating. Rick smirked as he watched the hat check girls fuss over the 'new guy'. A coy damsel, sitting at a front-row table, hurriedly stuffed a Camel into her cigarette holder and smiled in Matt's direction. Flirtatious eyelids fluttered as he drew closer. Rick shook his head when Matt embraced the young woman's bare shoulders and whispered, "Sorry, doll, I don't play with fire."

Her ruby-lipped smile fell with her shrug as he moved past her. She snatched the cigarette out of the holder, broke it in two, and tossed it into the glass ashtray on her table.

By this time, Matt was in the lead. They headed along the emerald green carpet, down the brick hallway disguised to mimic access to the kitchen and climbed the innocuous spiral staircase. At the top of the stairs, the Nest, where vampires and mortals imbibed, was disguised behind an innocent looking door marked 'storage'. To the right of that, stood Rick's office.

Rick drew the key out of his pocket and entered the silent, dimly lit room. Last night's receipts on his desk drew his immediate attention. Matt wandered to the bank of one-way mirrors that served as observation windows onto the dining room and dance floor. He'd been moodier since their encounter with the Moreau brothers.

"Something troubling you, dear boy?" Rick asked casually.

"Those two toughs, you think they're really gonna cause trouble?"

Rick shrugged. "They've been known to. They usually let their papa do the arm twisting. They're better known for their antics in Jamaica and Havana. Veronique was the girl who loved Hollywood glamor, but the family have made their fortune shipping bootleg and also peddling white slavery, cocaine, and heroin. I expect they want that building of yours because, if we scratched deeper, we'd find tunnels leading to the backroads. You, dear boy, are undoubtedly disrupting a very profitable business. No doubt they find you annoying. They'll probably cause a dust-up to get it back."

"Should I contact some friends on the force?"

"You know, with our family's growth in this area, we need a police force of our own. We have that in New York, Boston, and New Orleans. Until we bring the Responders here – something you might be interested in heading up – an assist from the local law could be helpful. You left the force without considering some on the night shift may not have a pulse."

Matt shook his head. "Absurd. Ridiculous."

Rick's brow rose. "You think so? I'll wager a box of Cubans you can find at least two family members among L.A.'s finest, which would be better all round for safety's sake."

"I'll look into it. Boy, will they be surprised to see me! They think I'm working at a movie studio."

Rick left Matt to contemplate the wisdom of vampire security as he ran the hand-cranked calculator to add last night's receipts. He was getting hungry. He'd finish this, and then suggest they sample the new B negatives in the Nest.

When Rick looked up, he found his protégé continually dropping and retracting his fangs, studying them in the mirror over the office bar. Rick passed him and slapped him on the back. "It never gets old, does it?"

Matt heaved an irritated sigh. "If they're so damn sharp, why can't I have a steak? I want a steak."

"Certainly. You won't taste it or digest it…" Rick gestured to the door and nodded, "…but shake a leg."

Matt stretched his neck. Rick noticed the fading contrast between Matt's formerly tan skin and his bright, white collar. "How do you know I won't taste it? I still have a tan."

"No, you don't. Are you basing your assumption on your fourteen days of vampire experience or my four hundred years?"

Matt's shoulders snapped up as he ran a finger around the inside of his collar. "What if I have *her* eat the steak?"

"Capital idea, dear boy!" He glanced down at the dance floor to see the debutante Matt dismissed on entry. "But don't start with her. You weren't very receptive when we walked in. You need to show her a little attention. A dance or two."

Matt rolled his shoulders and unbuttoned his suit coat. "Maybe she'd like to come up to the Nest for a drink? Of course, she is just a kid…"

"Oh no, my fledgling. No imbibing from her. She is the treasured daughter of the ersatz mayor of Hollywood. You'll show her a flattering, polite and chaste good time and send her home with a kiss on the cheek. If you behave, I have an excellent B negative awaiting your attention."

Matt's brow arched, a wicked grin spread across his handsome face. "And if I don't?"

"Well, then, I'm afraid you'll have a bottle of almost expired Red Cross blood."

Matt grimaced. "The citrate glucose taste is enough to discipline me."

"I'm glad to hear it. Go make Princess Hollywood smile. And remember, I can see you."

"Sure, Pops. I'm your guy." Matt ran both hands over his dark, pomaded hair and adjusted his pleated trousers. He turned at the door. "What if she rubs her knockers on me?"

Rick balled up the completed receipts and threw them at him. "No!"

****

Matt met Rick at the top of the spiral stairs. "Young ladies these days have too much moxie…" He smoothed his shirt and ran his thumbs up the back of his leather braces. "I knew she'd rub those cans on me!" He adjusted himself and shook his head.

"You should consider a jock to keep that thing tied down!"

"I suppose that's your technique?"

"A gentleman doesn't kiss and tell."

"I'm at the stage I want to bite and howl at the moon!"

"Poor abused vampire! Some hot blood will improve your mood." Rick didn't bother knocking but opened the door with his passkey.

The artist in Matt was impressed by the magnificent murals encircling the room. If the activity of feeding on mortals was not sensuous enough, the images of women dancing in diaphanous body-hugging dresses, gave his libido a boost. The painted characters swayed with near violent abandon to music coming from the white-coated orchestra painted on the far wall. The cut glass chandeliers spewed fractions of low light across the heavily engaged crowd in discrete booths.

Rick gestured him into a clam-shaped booth and sought the sommelier to escort his highly anticipated B negatives to their table. Twins, dressed identically to the nines, giggled, and followed the tuxedoed man to the booth.

"Ladies." Rick rose and bowed to them formally. "I'm Mr. Hiatt. Allow me to present my friend, Mr. Brenner." The girls giggled again. "Dear boy, meet Doris and Clovis O'Dell." He gestured to the two platinum blondes.

Matt, already on his feet at their approach, flashed his panty-dropping smile. "It's unfair of God to create two such exquisite creatures."

"Oh!" Clovis twittered.

"Won't you please have a seat?"

He waited for Clovis to slide into the booth as Rick did the same for Doris on his side and then both men bookended the lovely twins.

Doris whispered breathily. "Is it really true?"

Rick cocked his head. "Is what true, dearest?"

"Are you really, you know…creatures of the night?"

Rick's head bowed momentarily to dramatically rise, eyes opalescent and bright ivory fangs on display. His tongue danced from canine to canine. "You'll soon feel what these babies can do for you!"

The sommelier poured champagne into fine china cups. Matt smirked when he handed Clovis her cup and began a toast. She demurely dipped her chin and gazed at him through sooty eyelashes. "To the most delicious women in the City of Angels!"

"Oh, Mr. Brenner…"

Matt caressed her hand with a long, cool touch. "You have such a gentle hand, Miss Clovis." He dropped a kiss on her open palm. "I'll do my best to make tonight swell for you." Her mouth dropped open as Matt's nostrils flared at her pheromones. "I'll bet every inch of you is delicious." His cool palm skated up the slit in her satin dress to rest at the crest of her thigh.

If Matt worked to turn on his charm, he had to admit Rick's approach was effortless. He slid dangerously close to his platinum beauty, one long arm wrapped her bared shoulders as he bumped hips with her. "Your cache is delectable, Doris. I regret it's taken this long to meet you!"

The woman swooned against him. "You're too kind, Mr. Hiatt." Her bias-cut dress gaped slightly to reveal two magnolia smooth breasts with delicate rosy nipples.

He nodded at her allure and swept loose curls behind her ear with one long finger. Drawing close, his cool lips brushed the shell of her ear and sucked in a sample of her cologne. "I can see your pulse racing for me…" He drew his fingertip down her carotid and licked a line following the artery. "You aren't afraid, are you?" He drew her wrist out from her lap and his nose followed the path down the inside of her arm. Her flesh was flawless. "This is your first time." He buried his nose behind her ear. "You're a virgin." Doris blushed wildly, her pupils dilated. A smile spread from dimple to dimple. "I'll take care of that."

Before she could process his words, Rick found his mark, bit, and drew sensually against her throat. She gave two unbelieving gasps before she swooned into his embrace, shuddered in ecstasy, and melted into his lap.

Matt spent only a moment admiring his mentor's technique before he sank his fangs into Clovis' petite wrist. He felt the flush of her warm blood infusing him with life, appreciating again, the fact that vamps only warmed for four reasons: fight, flight, feeding and fornicating. He savored every swallow. Matt was about to finish the feeding, and if he had any say in it, this party for two would go horizontal. Shifting her body over his lap, his gaze met Rick's and his lips thinned in disappointment.

Rick broke his bite and spoke in a register too low for mortal ears. "Keep it all above the waist, dear boy. No hanky panky at the dinner table."

"How do you come up with all these stupid rules? I'm about to explode!"

"Another time, another place."

Matt grimaced and read Clovis's heartbeat. She was lost in erotic euphoria, beyond response.

Finished dining, Rick held Doris as he observed Matt seal his mark on Clovis's wrist. "These two lovelies need some pillow time, let's carry them to the lounge."

****

Matt found fully retracting his fangs impossible. He laid Clovis gently upon the chaise and when he straightened up, his trousers tented uncomfortably.

He felt Rick's assessing gaze. "Little problem, there, sport?"

"I have no small problems, these days. You said another time, another place. When and where?"

"We're headed there now…"

Matt's brow arched in curiosity followed by a heavy frown as a raucous clanging sounded throughout the building. "For the love of God, is that my woody alert?"

Rick's brow furrowed with concern. "It's the fire alarm. I'm hoping it's in the kitchen, but if the Moreaus are involved it could be anywhere."

"For Chrissakes!"

25

Rick turned to the sommelier and bartender. "Get the women out of the lounge, and everyone out of the Nest. We need to evacuate the building." He turned to Matt. "If you'll search the basement, I'll search the main floor. The kitchen staff is trained to deal with small fires. If it was there, they'd already have it out. The alarm continues, which means the source hasn't been found."

"Fire extinguisher?"

"At the top of the basement stairs, and another by the stage and the back door."

They abandoned the use of the staircase and jumped the rail, landing gracefully on the lower floor.

****

Pandemonium reigned in the ballroom as the crowd stampeded for the exits. Hector cupped his hands around his mouth and bravely bellowed from the stage as smoke billowed into the room. "Ladies and gentlemen, please remain orderly as you exit. Everyone will be safe if you stay calm." Sadly, Hector was ignored and the crowd all but trampled each other in the rush to escape.

Rick took only a moment to ensure the elegant vampire waiters poured water pitchers on tablecloths and whisked them out from under precious place settings. Glasses and silverware clattered to the floor as they threw the wet tablecloths over the heads of panicked patrons and guided them out the doors. Vampires, with no need to breathe, were not alarmed by smoke.

Leave it to the spineless Moreaus to employ flames from a distance against their enemies. Fire was the ultimate weapon against a vampire. When a blaze touched undead skin, there was no regeneration, the body turned to ash. Fire was their nemesis, and fire was Rick's target.

Rick steadied himself and with his extraordinary vampire perceptions followed the increasing sensation of heat to the cloakroom. There, the smoke was dense and black, and flames licked up the far wall. His vampire vision caught a glimpse of a white satin pump belonging to the coat-check girl. She lay out cold on the floor, blood oozing from a blow to her head.

Rick stood beside her instantly and had her in his arms and well on the way to safety. He passed the first coat rack when an explosion blew out the wall facing the street. Rather than relieving the smoke, the sudden change in air pressure blew debris toward them. Rick's immortal body was equipped to withstand the concussive blow, but Margery's frail mortal body was not. He felt the exact moment her spirit left her slight frame. Still, he held her as he staggered between the coat racks, inching toward the exit.

Rick heard the ceiling groan as the flames weakened its support, and he raced against time to make it out before the place caved in. Where were Matt and the rest of his staff? Had they made it out safely? That question was answered within moments when he heard Matt's voice shouting.

"Rick! Where are you?"

"Keep talking so I can follow your voice." The groan of the ceiling timbers escalated into load cracks, and Rick knew time was evaporating. He sprang through the air as only a vampire could, and landed beside Matt, the dead woman still in his arms. The two vamps lunged for the door, escaping just as a fireball blew out behind them and the roof caved in.

Rick reverently handed Margery's body into the arms of a policeman. Then Rick and Matt turned to watch his business burn to the ground. There was nothing the fire department could do except protect the properties surrounding him.

"Thanks for the rescue, dear boy." Rick sighed deeply and swiped soot from his face in charcoal streaks. "I guess the Moreaus were serious when they suggested the city would burn."

"Thank God you had the fire alarm, or there would have been a greater loss of life." Matt stripped off his ember-pocked jacket and threw it at his feet. "There'll be hell to pay, and the Moreaus will write the check."

4

Rick thought of Matt as he toweled off from a pre-tomb swim. Usually, he found swimming too energizing before going to ground, but this morning, he wanted to float, unwind tense muscles, and let the salt water of his huge pool dilute the odor of charred ruin, which apparently no soap would eradicate.

Matt suffered too much emotional trauma as a result of his rape turn. It was a miracle he'd survived two weeks. All Veronique's other victims were put down or ran screaming into the daylight within the first ten days. Well, everyone experienced turning differently. It wasn't as if Rick himself was exactly a 'consulted' turn. Tsura, the woman who turned him, the love of his life, never came out and said, "Your Grace, I'm about to make you immortal and lift you above petty mortal politics." What would he have done if she'd warned him? It wasn't as if he hadn't known there was something supernatural about her. Being raised in sixteenth-century Ireland, even as a nobleman, he lived in a time and place shrouded in superstition. Most of it was nonsense, but some of it… wasn't he un-living proof some of it was true?

His brother, the former Duke, inspired paranoia in Henry the Eighth. When Rick was named Duke after his brother's beheading, the king went after Rick's head, too. Henry's hunt for Rick, even after his disappearance, proved the wisdom of accepting Tsura's gift graciously. He would have been dispatched by the English crown as readily as many of his kinsmen were, notwithstanding he was Henry's man all along. If Tsura hadn't turned him, his life would have ended at the tender age of twenty-three and look at all he would have missed!

He lived a charmed, undead life mated to Tsura for over two hundred years, and in that time, he knew love and fulfillment he never believed possible. He couldn't say how he survived the last two hundred years without her. Life seemed impossibly long and empty. But now, now with the opportunity to do good for vampires and mortals alike, things were looking up. He supposed he couldn't ask for more; finding a mate who suited him as well as Tsura, would probably be impossible.

Rick was born a royal and received the finest education possible for the times. He was well versed in philosophy, languages, and history, interests he kept up to date. His cohorts, the mortal gentlemen of twentieth-century American aristocracy gathered at New York's Metropolitan Club. They might not see the parallels between the Seven Years War and World War I, but Rick had a living perspective.

Discernment and analytical thinking were his gifts. As a youth, he plagued the monks with endless theoretical scenarios. Clear thinking served him well through four hundred years of different incarnations. No, it wasn't vital in the management of a supper club, but that was not all he did. The Richard Hiatt of 1922 discreetly held an accumulation of wealth equaling the Astor, Vanderbilt, and Carnegie fortunes without the ability to rule in the daylight.

Rick was a member of the Vampire Council, a political involvement he felt obligated to sustain. As the undead population grew, they would become increasingly dependent on the rule of law. With his prior experience in governance and his close relationship with Benjamin Franklin, Rick was sagely qualified to help craft their legal code of conduct.

Fortunate to have been tutored by monks, he was a spiritual man, devout in the honor of God and His mysteries. When he discovered the principles of Jesuit education, he was especially drawn to the concepts of 'service of justice' and 'anticipatory joy'. It took two centuries for the joy to reappear after Tsura's death, but he sensed it increasing daily.

Without a beloved beside him, Rick acknowledged the benefit of true friendships. He experienced a new-found comradery and asked himself, *what's next?* For centuries he went through the motions, accumulating riches, but having no friends with whom to share them. He had dalliances, but no deep passion. He ran companies without emotional attachment. It was time to go deeper. It was time to let those around him see the real man behind the millionaire's image.

5

The following evening, Rick was without a club and a job, for now. Still, he didn't interrupt his nightly swim for anything, which was a good policy considering the negative news his insurance adjuster delivered. The athletic businessman loped alongside the swimming pool as he recounted the pathetic lack of evidence regarding the Tiki Club fire. The adjuster's slick leather soled shoes threatened to land him in the water beside Rick. "Mr. Hiatt, I'm not dressed for this exertion. Would you humor me by treading water while we finish this conversation?" The man mopped his forehead with a handkerchief.

Rick's pace through the water increased. "I'm killing time until my ward arrives." The Victrola in the corner began to drag. "In the meantime, would you be a sport and give that infernal machine a few cranks?" The music tempo picked up, and within three bars Matt Brenner entered the opulently lit indoor pool area. Matt's black satin pajama pants and robe were a contrast to the terracotta mosaic walls and patio floor. He blinked at the indoor pool's simulated daylight. His bare feet tread silently as he ran a lazy hand over his lightly furred chest. He yawned like the MGM lion and stood at the pool's edge. "You rang?"

While the insurance adjuster gave Matt suspect scrutiny, Rick waved a hailing hand. "Thank you for joining us, dear boy! This is Mr. March from California Indemnity. He's telling me there's been a rash of fatal fires. My Tiki Club was the first. They incinerated the Los Angeles Home for Widows and Orphans, the Children's Hospital and the Vista Movie Theatre."

"The loss of life has been staggering, not to mention the property."

Matt frowned heavily and ran his hands through his hair, sobering with the news. "Do they have any leads?"

"I'm afraid not; the mere act of extinguishing the fire destroyed potential evidence."

"What about the police, have they found any witnesses?"

"They've interviewed hundreds of people, but no one seems to have seen anything."

Rick climbed out of the turquoise tiled pool and slid into his terry robe. "Is their reluctance to give witness because of intimidation?"

"No. Every witness said it's as if the fires started spontaneously."

Matt turned away from Mr. March and handed Rick a towel. He spoke in sub-tones. "If they were moving at vamp speed, no one would see a thing."

Rick held the towel to his face. "Exactly." He placed a friendly hand on the adjuster's shoulder and guided him toward the door. "I trust California Indemnity has no doubts as to the validity of my claim."

"Oh, Mr. Hiatt, your reputation with us is sterling!"

Rick chuckled. "If you only knew how much those words mean to me." Matt raised a brow and buried a chuckle.

"Will you rebuild?"

"Certainly. And there will be significant upgrades. I'll be meeting with the architect this weekend. Eileen will see you out. Thank you, Mr. March."

****

"They targeted women and sick children?" Matt furiously downed two fingers of single malt and growled. His fangs dropped long and fierce.

"Dear boy, they have centuries on you. Your anger would be imprudent."

"We have to take a stand. Are you telling me you're not furious about this? You've talked about vampire cops – Responders? How do we get them here?"

Rick's bowed head shook. "I've already sent a telegram requesting immediate assistance. I'm guessing if they take the Sunset Limited, they'll be here in two or three days. Meanwhile, I have some ideas to thwart these cowards."

Matt paced in cop mode. "I can tell you right now, we need concrete evidence. If this went before a California court, it would be thrown out."

"We want them caught for crimes against vampires with Responder witnesses. Dress to impress and be ready in thirty minutes."

****

Venus's Fly Trap was located in Bunker Hill. Even the highly tuned Duesenberg chugged making the climb. But once there, the city of Los Angeles lay at their feet. There was scant time to enjoy the view after Rick announced their arrival into the speakeasy grille. The arched wood door swung open to reveal a velvet-draped rotunda.

"Good evening, Master Hiatt." A somber, tuxedoed butler stepped aside as he reached for Matt and Rick's hats. "Gentlemen, Mistress Venus is in your usual chamber." Matt raised a brow at the four dimly lit hallways feeding off the foyer.

Rick smiled mildly. "Thank you, Godfrey."

As Rick headed down the second corridor on the left, Matt shook his head. "Your *usual* chamber? Come here a lot?"

"On occasion. I believe you may be in for a treat. You did mention needing relief."

Matt stopped and looked up and down the hallway, and then hurried to catch up with Rick. "What are you getting me into?"

"Dear boy, mortal rules no longer apply to you." Rick paused, laying a brotherly hand on Matt's shoulder. He inclined his head forward and winked. "You're hungry, you're overwrought and overdue. Follow my lead."

"I'm used to taking care of these things alone with a woman. You're not planning to be there are you?"

"Look alert and learn." Rick stood in front of a heavy mahogany door and rapped twice.

An ingénue in black and white striped stockings and little else opened the door. Her maid's cap was larger than the bustier fighting to contain her creamy breasts. "Permission to serve you, Sir." Her blonde curls tumbled around her swan-like neck, as she stood, head bowed.

"Take us to your Mistress."

"This way, Sir."

As she led them away, Matt stared at the garter belt straps framing her bare derriere. "Is she dinner or dessert?"

"She's not on the menu. Listen, and learn."

The men found themselves in a temple-like room. Marble pillars flanked a raised platform with a rubine, velvet fainting couch. At Rick's arrival, the still figure lounging on her side, with her back to the room, slowly turned her head. Bias cut silk clung to the hills and slopes of her round figure. Her legs gracefully unfolded and delicate slippered feet poised to raise her from the fainting couch. Her jet-black bob glimmered in the low chandelier light. Matt's gaze riveted on her rhinestone beauty mark above passionate crimson lips.

"Master Hiatt, what's the chain of command?" Her chin was lifted, her voice haughty.

Rick slid out of his suit coat and began removing his cufflinks. "I say it, you do it, end of chain."

With those words, the woman stepped in front of Rick, starring him down, like a war of wills. After a beat, she knelt elegantly.

"All the way."

Venus gave a bored sigh and checked her manicure.

"What's… going on?" Matt shoved his hands into his trouser pockets. "Is this some kind of game?"

Rick's shirt was off, revealing his broad, muscled chest. His leather braces hung at his hips. "This is the best game, dear boy. Have a seat." He pointed to a chair in the corner. "Be a mouse. Relax."

The maiden girl guided Matt to an overstuffed chair and gestured for his suit coat. Matt shrugged out of it reticently in exchange for the crystal tumbler she delivered. He scented it, recognizing the A positive blood in the single malt. He sat obediently.

Rick's extended hand pointed to the floor. "Do I have your trust tonight, Venus?"

Her gaze followed Rick as he paced around her. "I was just teasing you, Sir."

Rick's nostrils flared as he took in an unnaturally deep breath. The voice that emitted from his lips was a deep, fierce whisper. "The Master does the teasing."

Venus held his gaze for as long as she could, as she slowly lowered her forehead to the floor, into a prostrate position.

Rick walked to the opposite wall and opened an armoire. Matt's gasp was audible.

"A proficient Master must gain his submissive's trust. Without trust, he is not the Master."

Matt's brows knit and froze as he considered Rick's words versus the items in the armoire. Rick slid out a drawer. After his hands ran reverently over several items, he chose a riding crop, a short leather flogger, a leather paddle and a bullwhip and laid them on an ornate trolley. Matt ran his finger inside his shirt collar and gulped the last of his drink.

Rick turned and regarded the prostrate woman and his own clothing. He summoned the ingénue with a beckoning of his fingers. "Your assistance is required in the dressing room."

Matt loosened his tie. "Me?"

Rick shook his head. "You stay where you are."

Matt opened his mouth to speak, found himself at a loss for words and closed it again.

I hope to God he's not naked when he returns.

He glanced at the woman on the floor. One flare of his nostrils told him she was undead and at least as old as Rick. The emotions rolling off her were pure joyous anticipation. Not a muscle moved. She stayed as commanded.

She likes this?

Rick emerged from the changing room in fawn riding breeches, English riding boots and nothing else. His warm brown hair was slicked back, and the skin of his arms, shoulders and chest gleamed with fragrant oil.

"What the…" Matt noticed the paddle Rick held casually at his side. Rick pulled the trolley with him as he walked purposefully toward the woman, Matt squirmed and leaned in.

"My sweet, is your safe word in place?"

6

"Fidelity," Venus murmured.

"Fidelity," Rick confirmed. "Very well." He struck his palm with a flat '*thwack*' and walked to stand behind her. "Don't be shy, Venus. Let everyone know how much you enjoy my licks. Present yourself." Her fine silk-covered ass rose proudly, and Rick took aim. The leather paddle whistled with momentum, announcing its arrival on her shapely buttocks.

Matt grimaced. Venus purred.

After swats from a few different directions, Rick's shoulders fell as he tapped the paddle against his chin. "Now, for something more invigorating. Venus, rise and strip. I want to see the glow of my work."

She rose promptly, head high. She shrugged off the thin straps of her gown and the silk melted to the floor.

Matt wasn't surprised she was now nude. Her figure was a fantasy of smooth, firm flesh. He squirmed at the sight her black bush.

Rick left the paddle on the trolley and released a lock on one of the wooden pillars to the left of the fainting couch. The wood opened to become an 'X'. "Hmm." Rick gave a devilish smile. "Do I tie you, or ask you to control yourself?"

She replied saucily. "Whichever you wish, Master."

Rick's gaze flashed fire. "You will work for your reward tonight, Venus. If you work hard, your reward will be… sublime. But, if this disrespect continues, you will be punished. Which will it be?"

Her smile challenged Rick. "We'll see."

"Oh, no, no, no. You will obey, or you'll be repentant."

"So, you've said."

Matt recognized this was meant to be some kind of playful banter, but the fun of it eluded him.

Rick swooped up the flogger from the trolley. "You will use the hand ropes to keep yourself upright." He indicated loops of rope hanging from the top portion of the 'X'. "Step up." Venus stared at Rick for a long beat, and finally, with a smirk, complied. Matt found himself clenching his jaw.

Rick walked to the front of the cross, facing Venus, his expression hard. "When I stand behind you, present your foot."

A shadow crossed her face for a flash of a second, and then composure returned. "As you wish." The woman bent her knee and lifted one leg to show Rick the sole of her foot.

'Swouf, swouf, swouf,' he snapped the flogger on her foot's arch.

Matt knew even for a vampire, feet were sensitive. He was sure of the pain, but if she felt it, she gave no sign. He scented the air – saline – tears – he wasn't crying, Rick wasn't, the ingénue had left the room. It was Venus. She was not crying but her eyes were watering from the sting.

"Change." Rick directed, and Venus obediently stood on the former as she raised her other foot for Rick's flogger. She shuddered slightly. "Now," Rick's voice was a low growl, "will we have a further show of rebellion, or will you obey?"

There was another moment of a standoff between the two, and Rick dropped the flogger and was in her face in a split second. In an angry subtone whisper between gritted teeth, he chastised her. "I brought my ward here to introduce him to the life, and your topping from the bottom is not appreciated." Venus's eyes widened as her gaze flitted from Rick to Matt and back. "I think you've forgotten how rewarding my praise can be, my sweet." He hissed. "And how empty my silence." His hand caressed her bright pink buttocks. "Ah… firm… warm… when you want to be." He ran his hand in a circle. She shuddered again, and Matt's vampire senses told him the reaction was no longer pain. This time it was arousal. "Don't you want my reward?"

Matt's eyes went wide, and he coughed, watching Rick's fingers sink into her folds. Now he didn't know where to look. She slid out of the wrist ropes, sinuously slithered down Rick's rigid body, and knelt obediently at his feet. Matt wiped his mouth with the back of his hand, unable to look away from their flagrant sensuality.

Rick paced slowly with the bullwhip still coiled. He dripped the end of the popper in tortuously slow patterns on her back and buttocks. He let the weight of the whip transfer from his hand to drag more heavily. Her breathy hum increased with his speed. "Your reaction shows me you want more."

"Yes, Master."

"Excuse me?"

"Yes, Master. I want more."

"Rise and assume the position." Matt covered his face with one hand, his fingers spread. When Rick paced toward him, he jerked upright. And his hands fell into his lap. "I'm not coming for you." Rick scoffed as he let out the whip. "You might want to move over there." He gestured to the other side of the room. Matt fairly levitated to get out of his way.

Rick's hand slipped through the strap, and his fingers embraced the braided handle. With a rotation of his shoulder, he began warm-up strokes. He worked his wrist and checked the length of his strike off to her right side. He took a step closer and winked at Matt. The whip sang through the air and Matt shuddered when he expected it to lay open Venus's pristine back. With each kiss of the popper, Venus's back bowed to meet the stroke. Instead of wounds, Matt watched a cross-hatching of pale pink stripes that increased with repetition to bright blushing welts. Her enjoyment increased with Rick's force until her body swayed in anticipation of the strike.

This is the oddest damn thing I've ever seen. And I've been to France.

When Venus's song became a near orgasmic wail, Rick dropped the whip. Matt scented the couple's arousal in the room's stunning silence. Rick headed to the cross and scooped Venus into his arms. She swooned as he carried her to the fainting couch. Holding her in his lap, he offered his wrist to her. Her drowsy eyes came alive with opalescence as her fangs dropped and she caught his wrist to her mouth. When she bit, her body thrashed with the orgasm and Rick pulled her length against his.

The ingénue was suddenly beside Matt. He'd missed her reappearance entirely. She took his hand. "Come with me, Sir." Matt followed but couldn't resist a look back over his shoulder watching Venus slide down between Rick's legs and begin unbuttoning his breeches.

****

The ingénue caught Matt's chin. "This way, Sir."

"You don't expect me to do that to you, do you?"

"Sir, with respect, Master Hiatt has been doing this for centuries. No one would expect you to do that tonight."

"Good. So…where are we going?"

"We're going to my frolic pad." She gestured toward a heavy door and withdrew a skeleton key from her cleavage. The room was lit with low lights, and resembled Venus's except a bed stood in place of the fainting couch."

"What's your name, anyway?" Matt paced the perimeter of the room as he removed his cuff links and unbuttoned his shirt.

She was on him in a flash, taking over his undressing. "They call me Luna." She slid his leather braces off his broad shoulders

47

and made quick work of removing his shirt, pulling the tail out of his trousers.

With Matt's hands free, his thumbs dipped into the top of her bustier and easily slipped both luscious breasts to fit atop the white garment. "Oh look, you can't be contained."

Her hand caught his trouser waist as her other hand stroked him through the wool. "Oh, neither can you." With a flick of the buttons, she had his slacks pooled at his feet.

He stood looking sheepish, hobbled by his trousers. "I've never been here before. What are the house rules?"

"There are no rules, we do what feels good." She knelt to untie his wingtips and he stepped out of his clothes.

"Well, then, let's move this party to that bed. It looks lonely there by itself."

"Will you allow me to pleasure you, Sir?"

"Ab-so-lutely."

7

Luna took his masculine hand in her dainty one and with a beguiling smile, led him to the bed. "Come with me. Please, get comfortable." Matt sank into the feather mattress with a satisfied groan, and stretched across the bed, enjoying the sight of her near nudity. He was astonished when, mid-stretch, the diminutive girl had both his wrists cuffed to the bedposts.

"Hey…what…"

"You'll enjoy this. Trust me. It's my job to bring you pleasure." Matt's smirk waned when she added, "Eventually."

His smile faded completely when he tested the cuffs. "These are the real deal."

She turned her pert rear to face him as she cuffed his ankles. When her task was completed, she knelt at his feet.

Matt watched his body react as the teasing girl unhooked her bustier. "I haven't been with a woman since I was mortal, two weeks ago. Once you move over me, I'm gonna be a two-pump chump."

His gaze followed her around the room as she dropped clothes and picked up small objects in her delicate hands. "Is that the way you want it?" She ogled his eager erection, waiting for attention. "You don't want this to end quickly, do you?"

"Being with you like this, I'm beyond control."

"Oh, I can help with that."

"I've never hungered like this. Every nerve is alive with need."

"It's your nature now. Every sense is heightened. You rest more deeply, taste more discerningly, and sex, well…" She chuckled.

"Has been a bust." He turned his face to the wall.

"Oohh?"

"The fangs work just fine. The wood is good, but there's no…" His voice dwindled to a whisper. "Mr. Happy never let me down before, but vampire life has killed him."

"I can bring him back to life." She smiled demurely, passing an item from hand to hand without revealing it.

"Oh, I can run the bases, just can't make it home." He gazed at his rigid erection bobbling with his words.

She shimmied closer and held up a strap of leather with heavy snaps.

"You're not helping right now."

She leaned over him and placed a finger to his lips. "Shh. No more talk." Sliding back between his spread legs, Luna licked the thin leather strip and warmed it in her mouth. Matt's gaze homed in on her pink tongue's excursion along the black strap. For the first time in days, he could feel a pronounced thumping in his chest. Deftly, she removed the leather from her mouth, wrapped it securely around the base of his pulsing penis and fastened the snap.

"Hey, …what are you…" She dragged her fingernails up his thighs to hook her thumbs under his sensitive sack. When he thought he was going blind from her simple touches, graceful fingers encircled his hard cock and her soft mouth descended upon him.

Matt's body was one great vibrating muscle. His lungs bellowed out his need. "Luna."

"Patience, Matthew. Everything comes to he who waits."

He writhed. "But some of us want to come soon."

Between the teasing strokes of her tongue, she posed the question. "You do know how all this works, now, don't you?"

"You're gonna lick me until my balls are blue."

"Oh, Matthew, Master Hiatt hasn't had the undead birds and bee's discussion?"

"I can't come. I…" His eyes clenched closed.

She held his rigid cock in both hands. "When you tried this alone, you didn't come, did you?"

"But I needed to."

Her strokes grew more insistent. "Of course, you did, and right now you think you're going to explode."

"I think it'll be another case of blue balls."

"You know why?"

"If I did, I wouldn't be in this shape. I'd come in here the confident cocksman I was."

Her thumb danced over the head of his cock. "Just one little secret will restore more confidence than you ever lost."

His moan echoed around the room. "Just do something, fast."

"You have to bite."

"Huh?"

"When you're ready to come, just let those fangs drop and bite me."

"That's it?"

"Uh huh. Once my blood flows, so will you. You can bite yourself when you're alone."

"I'm gonna throttle that son of a bitch, Hiatt. He *never* gave me a clue. I've been suffering, and he's been reading it. He's known all this time."

She straddled his hips, her hands softly stroking while she leaned forward, her delicate fangs out. "So now that you know the secret, why don't we enjoy ourselves?"

"Uncuff me, and we'll both enjoy ourselves." With a toothsome grin, Luna leaned her breasts on his face while she uncuffed his wrists. "Now you're talkin'." He reached for the cock ring.

"Oh, no, no. Leave our little friend in place. You'll thank me later." He threw his arms around her lithe body and buried his face in her breasts. "I can't get your ankle cuffs unlocked. until you release me."

"Just give me a minute here. Oh, doll, you are the cat's meow." His eyelashes brushed the sensitive skin on her nipples, and he let loose a throaty chuckle. "Daddy's home." With her in his arms, he scooted closer to the bottom of the bed. "Can you reach the cuffs now, because I'm not letting you go!" His skin connected with Luna's on an electric level and a shiver went up his spine. He felt alive to the roots of his hair. Her hands on his feet made him giggle. "That tickles!" He caught her and rolled her under him. "*Now*, Luna." His palm skated over her cleft and her wet warmth brought a crooked grin to his face.

"Ready to end that dry spell?" She teased.

He brought her dew to his tongue and moaned her name. With a swipe of his hand, he notched himself within her. "How about a trip to the moon?" He thrust home. His strokes deepened with each lunge. Grinding slowly against her mound, he angled himself to feel every sensation. He read the ecstasy glowing off Luna's alabaster complexion. That never happened as a mortal.

What a buzz this is!

Her pale hand slid between them, sending massive chills up his spine. She flipped off the thin leather strap, and sensation overwhelmed him. Pressure set his nerves on fire, and the release drove him to roll her over and pull her up to her knees. The sight of his thick cock splitting her pink flesh sent a rumbling growl through his chest. Grasping her hips, he thrust once, and felt the metamorphosis of his opalescent eyes and lengthening fangs. Bent over her back, he nuzzled her neck while he ground home within her. Her blonde hair parted, revealing his target and he bit.

As soon as her blood hit his tongue, his climax released. A hot tidal wave overcame him as every nerve in his body shook loose. The ecstatic swell coursed over him, tension released, liberating a flood throughout his body. He shook, clasped within her. Matt's arms wrapped around her as he rested his cheek on her shoulder. When his strength returned, he sighed, still pulsing within her, and lowered them both to the bed. Spooned on their sides, he cupped her breast and ran a fang over her earlobe. "That was outta the park."

8

Rick lay back in the corner of the chaise, his arm behind his head, one knee raised, and Venus draped casually against him. He smiled sardonically as she licked at his wrist, savoring the last vestige of blood.

"This is so delicious. Where did you find an A/B Negative?"

"I thought of you when I dined, I know it's your favorite." He sighed. "Won't be much more of that for a while with the Nest closed."

"Yes, I heard about the fire. I'm sorry. This week I've hired extra security. I turned away two men I didn't know."

"Well, that was the one prudent thing you did this week." He playfully spanked her buttock.

She pouted, unnaturally remorseful. "I was such a brat. I don't know what's gotten into me. When I heard about the fire and didn't hear from you, I was worried. Then you walked in here like the cock of the walk, I was delirious."

He drew her on top of him and cupped her face in his hands. "I *am* cock of the walk. Fire or no fire."

She sat on his lap and shrugged out of his hands. "You keep telling yourself that. I can't wait until you hit your next submissive streak, I will punish your fine ass."

He grinned. "You can try. Seriously, though, you saw my protégée, Matt Brenner. Luckily, Luna took him under her wing, because you, my dear bedfellow, probably have him thinking I'm a sadistic bastard."

"Well, you are a bastard some nights, but only sadistic every third Thursday."

"Nevertheless, he needs to learn the power exchange of dominance and submission, so seeing an obedient sub would get this fledgling on the right path."

"Oh, he is green, isn't he?"

"Yes, and you damn near scared him to death."

She shrugged. "How else will he learn how to deal with a brat?"

"He has to learn BDSM basics first. Let's lead by example. If your dominant side bristles at playing the sub, find me another sub." He tightened his hug around her shoulder and nuzzled her neck. "But you're so adorable, you know I enjoy playing with you." His tongue ran over her carotid. "I have a feeling he's a natural Dom if he gets into it. So, won't you help me bring him across?" His lips pursed at her ear and drew in a deep breath.

She shivered and shook. "You know that drives me crazy."

He chuckled. "Yes, I know."

"Alright," She offered her pinkie. "Pinkie swear, I'll be a good sub."

He hooked his pinkie and caught hers. "While I have your attention, I need your help."

Their gazes met, and she shrugged. "What now?"

****

"So, I can still come. Can I come often?" Matt nuzzled Luna's ear as he sank deeper into her.

"All you want. It's the vampire's gift to love long and love often. You have three more minutes to finish, or I won't be able to walk tomorrow."

Matt winked, and the tip of his tongue played at his bottom lip. His opalescent eyes closed, and his gleaming fangs dropped. His back arched, and he delivered a shuddering thrust. Luna presented her neck and with his instincts in high play, he bit. The second her blood touched his tongue he came with exquisite intensity. He heaved a sigh at completion and fell onto the bed pulling her close.

"What train hit me?"

"I'm glad you're enjoying yourself. You did ask about the rules of the house…"

"You said there are no rules…"

"I fibbed. I told you, we do what feels good…but that also implies we do it for each other…"

Matt rolled his shoulders and stretched his neck, a smile erupted. "Oh. Let me make amends." He delivered his finest crooked grin and pulled her to the middle of the bed. "What's sauce for the gander is sauce for the goose." He flipped over the handcuffs dangling from the headboard.

"Can I trust you, Matt?"

"I have the Good Housekeeping squeal of approval."

"I've never been given that guarantee."

He tightened the cuffs around her wrists, and she let him. "What's that stuff about a safe word?"

"If I cry Uncle, you stop, more about that later, I want to test that guarantee."

His tongue found every sensitive spot between her legs, and before long, Luna gave a series of squeals, approval and more. She was boneless by the time he uncuffed her and pulled her astride him. "Time for a ride."

"I can't…"

"Oh, but I know you want to. You're a vampire, you can do it. You are in the driver's seat, now, my dear!"

Slowly, Luna began to move, and as he felt her swell around him, Matt thrust harder and higher. She shuddered.

I must be hitting the right spot because she's not giving up.

He'd never been ridden so ruthlessly. Despite drawing from his past-due climaxes, her fiendish grinding began to yank his chain one more time. "You're a steam engine, Luna!"

Her head dropped back to show her neck and for the first time, he saw an alluring vampress in the throes of passion. Knowing he'd stirred her to this state whipped him to join her in the bite. She fell over him, still moving and her tongue plumped a thick neck vein without missing a beat. He could feel his own climax tingling at his root. With sensuous synchronicity, they bit and drew blood.

****

Matt emerged from Luna's chamber adjusting his necktie, leaning heavily on the door. His cool water bath and the charming attendants who scrubbed every fatigued inch of him had him up and ready for more. When he turned, Rick smirked at him from Venus's closed door.

"Those long legs of yours look a little rubbery, sport."

"You son of a bitch, you never told me about the bite! My legs would be in better shape if I'd been taking care of business these last two weeks."

"Didn't I? My mistake." Rick sank his hands into his trouser pockets. "You had too many other adjustments to face. If I'd told you there were unlimited orgasms, you'd never have come out of the shower." Matt slanted him a cutting smile. "Come along, time to be civilized."

"I'd zing you, but I'm exhausted." Matt shot Rick a satisfied grin as he smoothed back matinee idol curls with both hands.

"A little blood will set you right. I believe Venus has volunteers from among her serving staff, all worthy young women in need of financial help."

"Do they volunteer often? I'm willing to pay, but isn't it dangerous?"

"If you were one of Moreau's posse, it would be. We're civilized, and along those lines, I've had an idea." Rick opened the parlor door and the men found Venus and Luna, transformed into ladies of the house, not the evening.

"Gentleman." Venus's husky voice purred a greeting. She stood radiant in a white satin drop waist evening gown. Her slim hips were accentuated by the egg-sized ruby brooch at her hip.

Matt stared. "Please do join us. Would you care for some Champagne? I believe Luna has procured some delightful blood aspic canapes for our enjoyment.

Matt was in a societal whiplash. One hour ago, he was rutting like a stallion, and now everyone was dressed elegantly. The four looked as if they'd been reading Emily Dickenson and didn't know what anyone else looked like naked. He thought he was sophisticated. It was now obvious he knew nothing.

With some amusement, he followed Rick's lead when he placed a chaste kiss on Venus's cheek. "You look lovely tonight, my dear."

Matt crossed to Luna and took the bubbling coupe of champagne she offered. With a polite bend from his waist, he mimicked Rick's behavior from another night, his lips glancing the back of her hand. She giggled. He took his cue from the room before he drank.

When the four of them held their coupes aloft, Rick winked. "In honor of the loveliest undead in Los Angeles: I want to be naughty and still be nice. I want the fun without the price. I want the thrill of a long-drawn kiss. I want the things the virtuous miss. Now what I want is a little advice on how to be naughty and still be nice."

As the four touched their coupes, Venus smiled genteelly. "Very charming, my dear. Won't you have a seat?" She gestured to four tete-a-tete chairs in a square in the center of the room. She, Rick, and Luna, chose their seats facing center, and Matt followed suit. Four maids entered the room, and three sat on the other side of the serpentine chairs. One, Matt's chosen donor, hung back uncertainly.

"Good morning ladies. So good of you to share your bounty with us." Venus welcomed.

Matt eyed the clock on the mantle. No wonder he was hungry. It was three A.M.

Luna pressed small sherry cups into the hands of the volunteers. "Did you find your dinners satisfying?" As each of the young ladies accepted the sherry, they nodded and smiled. "This one kind act should fill your work card for the next fifty days. I hope you'll enjoy the freedom from daily drudgery. You could find this type of work the most satisfying."

"And not just monetarily," Rick added with a boyish grin. "If you're discrete, perhaps you'll decide to continue donating."

The lovely Latin beauty, who remained standing, dark eyes lowered, whispered, "I'm very uneasy, Sir."

Matt stood and bowed to her, gallantly drawing her into the chair beside him. "Don't be uneasy, dearest. I promise you, this will be pleasing. I would never hurt you."

"As you say, Sir." She viewed him through her coal black lashes.

"Please, trust me." He held each of her hands as she lowered herself into the chair.

Matt noticed Rick's gaze and a nod to Venus. He turned his attention back to the young woman beside him. "Why don't you try a sip of your sherry?"

****

After dinner, the couples adjourned to the wide back porch and the mild early morning air. They could hear the last of the

61

coyotes calling to the moon, and neighborhood dogs answering them as the rest of the city prepared for the coming dawn.

Rick leaned back on the railing and rolled his tumbler in one hand. "It's a given I will rebuild the club, but I'm imagining something more. Something I believe would profit us all."

Venus tipped a refill of the single malt into his glass. "I'm all ears." She winked at Luna.

Rick continued. "For a few decades, we've run similar enterprises. Matt, you've had your first taste of a lifestyle called bondage, dominance, submission, and masochism. For centuries it's been sequestered, but in this modern age, it's coming further into the light."

Matt smirked. "All my years on the force, how did I miss this?" He reached out to caress Luna's shoulder.

Rick shook a finger and chuckled. "Venus and her gifted women have catered to hundreds of fantasies, mortal and vampire. More enterprising mortals are discovering the advantages of volunteering to feed us. Prohibition, which will never last, has been a boon to my business."

Luna slid closer to Matt on the glider. "Prohibition seems to bring out the devil in all of us, it's certainly been a full-time job for me."

Rick grinned. "It occurs to me, we could combine our talents and produce a club that specializes in BDSM, hooch and blood. Ponder this. Most mortals, especially if unacquainted with our family, would be reluctant to give blood, despite the delight we know awaits them."

The others nodded, and he continued. "But subs... ah... submission under the hands of skilled vampire Doms, followed by sexual ecstasy... subs are our perfect audience."

Venus nodded with growing excitement. "You're absolutely right, Rick, male donors for us, female donors for you, all as members of an underground club."

Luna joined in the excitement. "Word would spread like wildfire within the undead and fetish communities. They would all pay *us* for their experiences."

Matt frowned, and leaned in, hands clasped between his knees. "There'd have to be a legitimate supper club above ground as a beard, the vampire club would be hidden below. Without that, the cops would begin sniffing around."

Rick nodded agreement, sat in an Adirondack chair, and leaned forward. "The Moreaus kill to feed, we would thrill to feed."

9

Rick swam laps as ideas for his new club blossomed in his mind. With each stroke of his lithely muscled arms, another layer of service and security for the undead sprung to mind. The new supper club would have twentieth-century safety features, all electric lights -- gas flames were not the vampire's friend. He needed a new name for a new supper club. The Tiki Club was ashes. Out of its flames would rise The Phoenix. *Yes, The Phoenix. That's a good name.*

What will we call the BDSM club burrowed deep underground? A name like The Nest, implied comfort and coddling, the last sensation sexual submissives desire.

What about The Fetish Fortress? Meh... It's bondage... bastion... Bastille...The Goaler!

The uninitiated would think it was to celebrate soccer. He had to remember these names. Regardless of the name, it would be an undead paradise, assuming they could eliminate the threat from the Moreaus. He received a return telegram from the Responders in New Orleans, asking him to meet their arrival on tomorrow's evening train.

Today, he and Matt would meet with the developer from San Francisco who would mastermind the financing and construction of this lofty venture. From all reports, Adam Lachlan was something of a monetary magician, bringing together epic structures and discrete financiers. Everyone marveled at his business acumen at such a young age, and Rick chuckled, the same had been said of him for centuries.

I need to check him for a pulse.

Rick climbed the ornate stairs out of the pool and glanced at the large stone clock over the massive decorative fireplace. It was approaching six o'clock, and since Matt had not made an appearance as yet, he needed to roust him off the slab.

With a trot through the pool's changing room, Rick slid the towel shelves aside and took the steps down two at a time to the subterranean level. At the bottom, hallways ran from a central lounge, like spokes, to end in nondescript doors. Each door guarded a personal mausoleum. Who cared about the number of bedrooms in a vampire's mansion? What counted was how many mausoleums they could accommodate.

Rick rapped 'shave and a haircut' on the door, with no response. He pressed an ultrasensitive vampire ear to the door. Nothing. Rick chuckled at the memory of his rubbery-legged friend when they returned before dawn this morning. He threw open the door to see Matt reclined, arms crossed over his muscled chest, still dead to the world.

Rick walked up to Matt's ear and whispered, "Wakey, wakey. Hands off snaky!" With the abrupt command, Matt instinctively threw his hands down to cover his twig and berries.

"What the hell?" Matt bellowed as his feet hit the floor.

"Time to be up and about, dear boy! I've already swum a mile."

"When I'm a damn merman, I will too."

"Estelle left you a cup of blood to jump-start your evening. We have to meet this Adam fellow, on Wilshire at seven. There's a prime piece of property I want to snap up before someone else grabs it."

****

Matt's handsome face screwed up in distaste as he turned a circle in the middle of a mostly deserted stretch of Wilshire Boulevard. "It smells like tar. How is this prime real estate?"

"The long game, remember? One day this city will spread from Bunker Hill to the coastline, and this spot will be worth millions."

Matt's gaze bounced from oil well to oil well across the street. "It's like fifty metronomes clicking to different beats. This is going to get on my nerves."

Matt saw the impossibly tall blonde man carefully stepping through the lot. "Is he on the level with this property?"

Rick scrutinized the man in the pinstripe suit. "I hear in the next few years, this will be a park, the oil rigs will be gone, and we'll be across the street." He pointed east. "Prime real estate."

"And you know this, how?"

"Friends with information."

Adam stepped up to the men and offered his hand. "Adam C. Lachlan, developer and rainmaker."

Rick offered his hand in return. "Richard Hiatt, club owner, and this is my partner, Matthew Brenner." Rick held onto the handshake an exceptionally long time, feeling the man's warm hand as well as his pulse.

Definitely not a vampire.

He glanced at the cafe frequented by the oil workers. "Can we find a place to sit and talk?"

Adam's brow rose. "If you'd care to follow me, I know a comfortable spot, not far, where we might even find some refreshment. If we come to an agreement, we can celebrate."

****

Matt drove as Rick studied the architectural drawings. "I think the underground area needs one and a half times this space."

They followed Adam's yellow Daniels Speedster as he swerved through traffic. Matt laughed. "Ah, Rick, I have a feeling I know where Mr. Lachlan is headed."

Rick glanced up as they chugged up Bunker Hill toward Venus's Fly Trap. Had it not been known as a joy house, it would be the perfect haunted house, gabled and Victorian. Rick's boyish grin grew knowing. "I wonder what Mr. Lachlan's fetish is?"

Matt shook his head. "Not my business; I don't want to know."

"Embrace your nature, don't hold onto your silly mortal constrictions. I have a feeling Mr. Lachlan could be an asset to us in more ways than one."

****

Once again, Rick and Matt found themselves in the parlor. Venus greeted Rick and Adam as longtime friends. She hadn't heard the verdict on Matt from Luna who was still dead to the world.

What is it about Matt Brenner?

Venus paused graciously at the door to the parlor. "Gentlemen, I must mentor a few new guests. If you need me, send Godfrey."

Godfrey stepped forward. "Refreshments, gentlemen?"

"I'm particularly fond of strawberry wine if you have any." Adam smartened his sleek blonde hair in the mirror over the mantel. He was uncommonly handsome, even Rick could see it, and by God, he was a Viking of a man. He wore his uber-blonde hair parted on the side and swept back with a dab of pomade. He looked positively bulletproof with his aqua blue eyes. At six-foot-six, he towered over Matt and Rick.

Rick observed Matt watching Adam from under his eyelashes as Matt played with his pocket watch. Rick winked at him over the strawberry wine comment. "Godfrey, something a little more substantial for Mr. Hiatt and me. The single malt with the pomegranate, please." Godfrey bowed and exited the room.

The three men took each other's measure. Alone again, they poised over the serving tray. Adam smiled wryly as Rick opened the cut ruby glass decanter, nostrils flaring. Holding the artful vessel out to Matt, he commented, "How zesty!"

Matt shrugged with a humorous smirk. "Sure, if you say so."

Adam watched the red fluid infiltrate the single malt in their glasses. "Whenever I take Venus's company for the night, she

69

drinks the same combination. Is pomegranate the secret to her stamina?" His raised his strawberry wine to begin a toast.

Matt turned his head and winked at Rick, who was not particularly amused. "You enjoy her company for the night? How often?"

Rick's face lost all humor.

"I arrange to stay here whenever I'm in town. It's generally three to five days a month. I was lucky she had the room to spare, this week. I was due in yesterday, but she had no vacancies."

Rick raised his glass, but his smile didn't reach his eyes. "Venus has always had an extraordinary work ethic."

Adam raised his glass. "I'll drink to that!" His lips curled in a wicked smile after he swallowed his wine.

Rick drained his glass, watching Adam closely, and without looking at Matt who was pouring his own drink, he held out his glass for more.

"Please, let me serve you." Matt clipped sardonically.

"Let's get down to business, shall we?" Rick brusquely led the men to a dining table, buried under blueprints.

****

When Venus returned on her own, hours later, the three men were heads down, pouring over the plans. Adam raised his architect scale ruler and shook it at Rick. One frustrated hand ran through his hair. Adam was deconstructing before Rick's eyes. His necktie open, he walked in his stocking feet, sporting loud argyle socks. "This won't fit on the property you want... You'll have to buy the larger parcel across the street at four times the price."

Matt walked away from the table. "God, no, the whole place smells like tar. They should pay us to take it!"

Adam rolled back his cuffs and leaned on one palm. He pointed with his pencil. "Here, across the street, it's twice the footage. You'd get the larger underground as well as a deeper lot. Plus, there are no wells there now. Once financing is secured, everything's jake."

Rick leaned back against the mantel and closed his eyes in thought. "I admit you raise a valid point." He reopened his eyes and smiled at Venus, the first of the men to acknowledge her. "Venus, my dear, this is your project as well. Do you have any requests?"

Adam's head snapped up. "Venus? You're part of this?"

Venus posed proudly, hands on hips. "Boys, how many hours and how many bottles of strawberry wine has Godfrey delivered? This is how far you've come?"

The men watched her warily. Rick offered with a shrug. "We've agreed on the rough dimensions and the change of parcels."

"If we're becoming partners, we can't afford misunderstandings. All the cards are going on the table, now."

Rick visibly bristled. Adam paced a small circle as he complained. "The underground portion is totally out of scale to the rest of the building."

Venus led him back to the table and pointed a long nail at the unmarked room. "The underground is the reason for the building."

Totally exhausted at two A.M., Adam dropped his ruler. "You can build a speakeasy on a ground floor. We'll use hidden doors—"

Venus sidled up to Adam and caught each end of his open necktie, sliding it back and forth under his collar. She smiled beguilingly. "This will be a little more than a speakeasy. It will also contain fetish suites, private and public, we'll have a lounge, restaurant and bar."

"My dear, I believe you're overestimating the area's interest in BDSM. While your house has proven profitable, the kind of space you're describing here would demand a huge market, far greater than your current clientele." Adam scoffed and walked from the table. He picked up a near-empty bottle of wine and swallowed the last of it. He sat resignedly, with one long leg crossed over the other.

"Adam, have you ever heard of vampires?"

He stretched his legs before him and wiped at his face. "I do read, Venus. Yes, I've heard of those bloodsuckers." He chuckled with his hands behind his head, aqua eyes dreamily half closed.

"I'm a vampire, Adam."

He dropped his hands on the chair's arms. "Applesauce." He quirked a grin.

With an invisible rush, Rick and Matt flanked her in front of the doubting man. "Please don't think we're ganging up on you." The three dropped their heads and when their transformation was complete, down to the icy, pale skin, Adam was on his feet.

"I may have been hasty in my response." He acknowledged calmly as he scrutinized Rick and Matt's translucent features.

"You're taking this extremely well, old boy," Rick observed.

"We all have our secrets…"

Rick and Matt exchanged raised brows.

Venus took control again. "I tell you this, so you'll understand. We have a submissive clientele willing to feed us for the sexual thrill of our bite. It only makes sense for us to capitalize on the vampire's natural dominance."

Matt approached Adam looking more miserable than menacing. His already pale complexion faded to parchment. "Two and a half weeks ago, I was pounding the pavement as a Los Angeles detective." He pointed dejectedly to his fangs. "One bad date and I end up like this." His melancholy gaze met Adam's. "There's a family of vampires by the name of Moreau who lure mortals to their deaths. Unfortunately, I dated one of their shills. I took a gal out for a steak dinner and thought we were going back to her place for some sheet time. Instead, I was dessert for a vampress who drained me, turned me, and thought she'd make me her pet."

Adam frowned, feeling sympathy for the vampire's obvious grief over his lost mortality.

Rick picked up the story. "The Moreaus are known for their criminal deceit. In Matt's case, Veronique Moreau performed what is called a 'rape turn', which I'm sad to say she's done many times in the past. This time, there were an abundance of witnesses, and I managed to rescue him. Veronique was prosecuted, sentenced, and escaped with her family's help. She turns men without intentions of training them to be citizens of the vampire family. Had she kept him in her harem, he would have become an abandoned, murderous rogue. Ultimately, he would have been put down, and there would have been numerous unsolved murders in his wake."

"So, Veronique is the criminal in her family?" Adam questioned.

"No, Veronique is one of the villains in a family of criminals." Matt clarified. "When her financial assets were granted to me by the Court, her brothers bid on the property which was her speakeasy and mash pad. When I refused to sell to them, they threatened 'the city will burn'."

"I've been reading about the catastrophic fires all over town. You think these Moreaus are behind it?"

Rick nodded. "We know they are. We have what amounts to vampire G-men coming into town tomorrow to investigate. The sad truth is the Moreaus are responsible for ninety percent of the city's unsolved murders."

Adam shrugged. "I thought all vampires were killers."

"That hasn't been true for centuries. Most vampire-related deaths, nowadays, are accidental." Rick countered.

"A steady food source means we're no longer driven mad with bloodlust." Matt lifted his glass with enthusiasm. "Rick has identified a population who are eager to provide us with donor blood. Hell, they thank us for it. We'll have 'em lining up around the corner."

"It's that good?" Adam was skeptical.

Matt winked at Adam. "Aw, c'mon, Venus has never bitten you?"

Adam's eyes went wide, and he turned to her. One hand covered his fly. "That's our magic?" His finger pointed back and forth between them. "I thought it was just us."

Venus covered her grin. "In a way…it is."

Adam looked down at Rick with a Dominant smirk. "It *is* the bee's knees."

Rick reached out and smoothed Venus's glossy ebony bob. A low growl rumbled in his chest.

Standing between them, Venus pressed them farther apart with the flats of her hands. "Gentlemen…" She warned.

Matt laughed outright. "Is it time to drop trousers and measure?"

The challenged men split to opposite corners.

Adam muttered. "Of course not."

"I don't know what you mean." Rick mumbled, and then added in subtones, "Mine's bigger."

Matt handed him a tumbler and nodded. "Okay, Pops." Matt returned to the table. "Now that we all have an understanding of the purpose for the underground section, let's continue with the plan."

****

By four a.m., their moods mellowed. They threw open the tall parlor windows and the garden's moonflowers perfumed the room. Cigars were produced with even Venus taking a celebratory puff. Everyone agreed to the plans. The Victrola belted out Eddie Cantor, and laughter peppered their conversations for the first time.

A luscious honey blonde swept in, and made a beeline to Matt, plopping into his lap. She purred. "I see you've returned to the scene of our crimes of passion!"

Rick rolled his eyes and Adam smirked. Venus walked over and gracefully embraced her. "I was beginning to believe he bewitched you."

Matt caught her around the waist and bounced her on his knees. "That's a question of who's bewitching whom?"

Venus nodded at Adam. "Luna, I don't believe you've met Master Lachlan. He'll be staying with us for the next few days." Rick's gaze cut sharply to her with her use of the title. "Master Lachlan is joining in our venture with Master Hiatt."

Matt's confusion over the use of 'Master' bubbled up. "What am I? An apprentice?"

Luna wrapped her arms around Matt and giggled. "You can be whoever you want."

****

If Rick had been paying attention, rather than enjoying the fun, his heightened undead senses would have heard the hiss of the gas and the scratch of the match. But the Victrola and the congenial sport lulled him into distraction. He had no more warning than the others. One moment they were laughing over a Cantor lyric, the next he was flying, ass over elbows into the rose garden. The force of the blast still rang in his ears. He shook his head and looked up. The entire mansion was consumed in flame, and within the conflagration, the walls and roof collapsed upon them. He stood, shakily, looking for Matt and the others.

"Hey, we're up here." Matt pulled leaves and twigs out of Luna's hair before they gracefully dropped the twenty feet to the ground.

Adam yelled as he fought Venus's vampire strength. "It's no good, sugar."

Rick was on Venus with his added preternatural strength. "You'd be ash." He held her fast. "Venus, baby, look at me. There's nothing you can do."

The wall of heat forced them into the street before the fireman's bell was heard moving closer. Venus collapsed into Luna's arms as they encircled her.

Rick stood defiantly, glaring at the fire. "They want war? I can be extremely civilized. They'll never see it coming."

Adam wiped wood debris from his face. "This was a gas explosion."

Matt shook his head. "Don't count on it. The Moreaus did it."

Rick brushed off his tattered trouser legs and began pulling debris off his car. "Everybody, back to my place. There's no victory without a plan."

10

Rick and Adam spent the day concocting fabricated financial documents. The millionaire Moreau family was about to nosedive into a tenuous financial spider web of insolvent credit. "Of course, within two days, Papa and his devil's chorus will succeed in discrediting this account," Rick said, "but while we need it, Samuel and Jonas Moreau should find it impossible to finance a night in a flophouse."

Adam riffled through the documentation and chuckled. "You know, I have no idea where vampires sleep."

Rick sat back and lit a Cuban cigar, and after taking a long draw, he smirked. "We don't sleep, we go to ground."

"Dirt?"

"No, any dark, cool, secure place. The brothers are undoubtedly in a posh hotel ordering trolley after trolley of ice, daily, to fill their bathtubs."

"Ice?"

"Yes, it's pleasant to soak in ice from dawn to dusk when we're away from home. In the past, we sought out basements in the cities and caves and wells in rural areas. We're dead, our bodies degrade in heat. At dawn, my marble catafalque is refreshing."

Adam shook his head. "And you sleep?"

"Our minds go dark and we're dead to the world."

Adam grimaced. "So, the brothers?"

"They have no friends to house them, so they fill the tub with ice, lock the door, turn out the light and go to ground."

"Ah." Adam nodded, and Rick felt his scrutiny. "So, you sleep in your basement?"

Rick grinned secretly. "I have a place."

Adam shook his head. "Okay, but you have elegant bedrooms here."

Rick's lips curled boyishly. "Bedrooms are used for other things too. You can do anything in a bedroom."

"None of my beeswax." Adam raised his hands in faux surrender. "So, I assume you have someone inside the bank to pull this off?"

"Ab-so-lute-ly. I have magicians on it right now. Moreau dollars will pull a disappearing act."

Adam gave him the fisheye. "Abracadabra?"

"No, red ink. In a few days, it will be discovered as an error. But in the short term, it will wreak havoc."

"I can't imagine the Moreaus will be especially pleased by this."

"No, I imagine they'll be vexed and off-kilter, as we want them."

Matt entered the room in a rush of enthusiasm. "I just spoke with one of our family members on the police force. The Moreau bootlegging business has a fleet of motorboats to move their hooch up the coast. And a mother ship from Mexico berthed in international waters off San Diego." Matt was a man exhilarated by tracking his prey. "They frequent a series of caves in La Jolla, probably used as warehouses. Between the caves and the tunnels leading from the Sunset Grande, we should be able to plant some artifacts that will intrigue them."

Rick slapped his friend on the back. "Excellent work, dear boy. Do you believe we can surveil the Moreaus around the clock?"

"Consider it done, Pops. They won't bite the air without us knowing about it."

Adam stood and stretched. "I'm heading over to the Sunset Grande now, with a large construction crew. We'll basically move dirt and shrubbery from one spot to another, not much actual work, but a lot of activity. They won't be able to miss it."

"Good man. We appreciate you handling the day-work."

Rick's enthusiasm faded, and he rubbed at the emerging feeling of unease in his chest. The part of their plan he could neither anticipate nor control fell to Venus and Luna. Despite his confidence in their abilities, he worried for their safety.

****

Rick's fortune originated in his European roots, and when he landed in 1760 Philadelphia, he made astute investments in the city which fostered his greatest opportunity. As a mortal Duke, Rick supported Henry VIII. Seeing the capricious nature of the monarchy, he sought out friendships with Philadelphia's revolutionaries. Benjamin Franklin really knew how to woo the bourgeoisie. With a steady diet of wealthy skirts and business connections, the enterprising vampire flourished in his new country. His estate rivaled any Newport real estate, and most of the minor principalities in Europe.

The Responders were received in some of the finest castles and estates in Europe. Their brethren vampires in the United States, though often more affluent than the average citizen, didn't have the age-old network of wealth. Thus, the New Orleans Responders were respectfully impressed and a little awed by Rick's luxurious trappings and old-world command.

The gazes of Chief Inspector LaTour and his subordinate, Inspector Paquet, followed Venus avidly as she passed them single malt along with the business documents. Rick kept his amusement to himself. What did Ben Franklin say? 'A pretty face engages the mind.'

"The Moreaus have left mortal carnage in their paths for decades."

Chief Inspector LaTour, a reedy man with an intricately waxed mustache, flared his nostrils with tempered dismissal and fixed Rick with a piercing blue gaze. "Mortals are cattle."

Rick continued as if LaTour hadn't spoken. "As the mortal world becomes more sophisticated, they'll know us by the wounds we leave unless we're extraordinarily careful. The Moreaus are careless, and their carelessness will paint us all with the same brush. Unfortunately, it doesn't stop there. We have convincing circumstantial evidence they are now targeting vampire family ventures."

LaTour shrugged. "That's the rub. Circumstantial evidence is not enough."

Matt stood to his full height in top-dog posture. "In my police detective experience, we cannot dismiss the corollaries entwined throughout this evidence. It's true, we need verification, but that's a matter of following the clues. They threatened us, and the initial fire was at Rick's Tiki Club. Their next targets were the Women's and Children's home and the Children's Hospital, both heavily supported by the Hiatt Charitable Trust. Rick was their greatest competition, and they eliminated the business and services he valued. But they haven't stopped there. Last night's attack on Venus Aquillius's home and business left several upstanding vampires and mortals immolated.

Inspector Paquet, who listened the entire evening without comment, raised his head from introspection. "With due respect, Chief Inspector, before you came to New Orleans, we had a similar pattern in 1917 when Francois Moreau 'negotiated' for the Storyville Nest. He cited an ancient land grant from a distant relative and when the Vampire Council sided with the current owners, burned his way through town. He took over the disputed property, and your predecessor was torched. They are mercenary, these Moreaus."

LaTour threw up his hands. "The New Orleans event means nothing in this discussion."

Rick was at LaTour's throat instantly, fangs gleaming in the light. "How many of us have to die? How many innocent mortals will be slaughtered? Your lassitude with our evidence, although circumstantial, is unsettling." Rick turned from the Chief Inspector and drew his fingers through his tousled hair. "Do we wait until they come for you?" Matt joined Rick and drew him to the other side of the room to a chair and poured a drink.

Venus's gaze narrowed as it swept the room. "I have to confess I find your reluctance suspect. Do we scratch a LaTour and find a Moreau sympathizer? I would hate to think that I must take this above your head to Europe."

LaTour harrumphed indignantly. "I see Los Angeles vampires hold little regard for the law. Come along, Inspector Paquet, we're returning to New Orleans." He stood and waved a commanding hand.

Paquet shook his head and stood, hands on hips. "Sir, you file your report, I'll file mine. I see sufficient evidence of criminal activity. The Moreaus threaten the thin veil between mortals and the undead."

"You're disobeying a direct order?" LaTour stuck his thumbs in his vest pockets.

Paquet mirrored his posture. "Sir, my experience with this family tells me these complaints threaten every one of us."

LaTour dug into his breast pocket for his notebook, licking the end of his pencil, he furrowed his brow and his lips moved silently. Rick skirted the two vampires and whistled. "I can cut the tension with a knife."

Venus checked her hair in the mirror and pinched her cheeks, and then turned on her heel. In LaTour's face, she came up to his chin. Shaking her head in silent judgment, her hand disappeared into her skirt and withdrew a walnut handled, silver stake. The sucking sound of it penetrating through clothing and undead flesh echoed in the silent room. The men stepped back, and the lone non-vamp in the room charged forward to see what she'd done.

"Good God, woman! Is he dead?"

"Undead, for some time, I believe. He'll take advantage of a quiet mausoleum in Rick's chambers, and when he rises, let's all hope we were right."

Matt scratched at his jaw as Venus lowered the vampire to the floor. "Can he hear us?" He walked closer in fledgling curiosity.

Rick chuckled and shook his head. "My dear, you are the deadlier of the species."

Venus looked smug and dusted her hands. "Somebody had to do it. The conversation was going nowhere."

11

Adam shut the door on what was a sumptuously appointed guest bedroom. Ironic, in that Rick and his vampire guests apparently never used the bedroom for sleeping.

When did life become so complicated? How have I lived nine hundred years without meeting a vampire before? Well, maybe I have and didn't know it. Mother told me I was self-centered. Am I really that oblivious?

Adam walked to the armoire and marveled at the wardrobe Rick's haberdasher sent over with barely a day's notice. He needed to replace everything he brought with him from San Francisco; it was all obliterated in the explosion at Venus's Fly Trap. Now, Adam had three of everything he needed, and he was not an easy man to fit. Being six-foot-six with shoulders and muscles of herculean proportions, he didn't dress off the rack.

"This is Hollywood, old man, they are used to whipping up a wardrobe in a hurry." Then Rick's lips curled into a bawdy smile. "They did call back to confirm your rise and inseam."

Well, that was snarky.

Still, he found his new vampire friends very likable. To be honest, he liked Venus since they met two years ago. Who would ever have suspected she was undead? Matt explained their cold bodies warmed up nicely for sex. Adam supposed it was a kind of compliment that she was warm whenever they were together.

Why can't I remember feeling the bite? All I remember is being pulled under a wave of ecstasy.

His hand ran to the crook of his neck, and he contorted to see his back in the mirror. He couldn't get the right angle. Grabbing the shaving mirror, he held it and angled farther back. There, reflected in the bathroom mirror, were a few spots that could have been equally distant freckles. Adam didn't have freckles. When he brushed his fingertips over the spots, his spine tingled. With a bit more pressure, the sensation amplified, and it was not unfamiliar. Venus always made his spine tingle. Now, he knew why. Venus incited memories of his youth when his dragon was always ready to rut.

Not since his salad days, when he was green in judgment and fresh with the fairer sex, did he know as much pure enjoyment in a bed. His doleful experiences in outliving mortal sweethearts left him wary of any involvement leading to love. If he knew Venus was a vampire, an immortal, would he have been more attentive? No. There was an enjoyment between the two of them, but no spark. And honestly, the thought of lying nightly with a stunning dead woman was not as appealing as one might imagine.

It was rare for a shifter, especially a dragon shifter, to live in the mundane world. Dragons were clannish; they kept to themselves in isolated areas. If he were still in good graces with dragonfolk, he would have spent his two-year period of 'reflection' in the mortal world and returned home to mate, raise a family, and contribute to the clan. That one fateful night with the fair Princess Belinda, who was intended for the Prince of her clan, had damned him to banishment.

One hundred years later, if he went begging to another clan, he would probably win entry to their lowest caste. They wouldn't turn him away—after all, he was a Flight's End Royal—nor would they allow him more than a peasant's life. His current self-worth was too brittle to tolerate that kind of sacrifice. No, for now, he would remain in the mundane world.

His marked successes across the young country of America invigorated him. As his perennial thirty's appearance became an issue within a mortal community, he moved and assume a new persona. It was thrilling to amass a fortune, study at the finest universities, become a shipping magnate; a lawyer affiliated with the Underground Railroad, a successful gold prospector in California and now, an accomplished land developer. None of these would hold sway with his clan. They had long memories and low tolerances. He supposed he never was the model son and Prince by dragon standards.

Now, he was looking for new territory to explore, perhaps the territory of the psyche? In today's world, a journey into the mind was possible. He was eager to explore his own deep motivations and those of others. Maybe in helping himself, he could share the ability to overcome emotional pain. One evening's conversation with Matt convinced him every soul grappled with some kind of mental torment.

The walls between mortals and paranormals were crumbling as the world's population grew. Though mortals outnumbered magicals, there was a danger of sinister magicals gaining the upper hand. One would think vampires were not inclined to care for mortals. However, Rick and Matt were pioneering mortal safeguards, protecting them from unnecessary death. True, it was like a rancher protecting his herd to continue eating, but it was also more. Rick and Matt saw injustice in their vampire community and worked to right the wrongs.

Adam, uninformed about other magicals and cut off from dragon kind, blended only with mortals. Burying one love after another wore on him. If he couldn't stop falling in love, perhaps a wedding ring would be a flashing beacon to warn off women. If he forgot and took a shine, the woman would dismiss him as a philanderer and cut him off.

Yes, let them help me.

For the first time since his banishment, Adam felt he was among kindred spirits. This bolstered his soul. Moving within this paranormal milieu, Adam knew his strange life would forever intertwine with other magicals.

As he toweled off and slid naked between the finest linen sheets he ever enjoyed, his head rested easier on the downy mountain of pillows. Adam closed his eyes and reckoned it would all be copacetic.

12

A battalion of bellboys followed The Beverly Hills Hotel manager as he descended on the Moreau brother's bungalow. With a furtive look over his shoulder at the manager, the head bellman knocked on the door. Nothing. The manager nodded with a raised brow. "Go ahead. Knock again." Nothing.

The young senior bellman blanched white and shrugged. "Nobody home, Sir. We could enter and pack their belongings."

The manager took a step back. "Gentlemen make haste. These young men have been trouble from the moment they checked in. The amount of ice they've required burdened the Polo Lounge. They are not good tippers. Mr. Anderson wants them gone at the first opportunity." He waved the luggage cart to the door as his senior bellman produced a key and entered.

The luxurious bungalow was shrouded by closed blinds and draperies. The bathroom doors were closed, but the bedrooms were untouched. The bedspreads and pillows had nary a crease.

As the six bellboys headed into the two bedrooms and the closets, the bathroom doors burst open, bouncing off the walls. From two directions, the nude vampires, Jonas, and Samuel, raged toward the intruders. Their eyes burned like fire as they cursed piercingly in French and moved with supernatural speed.

The manager stood in the living room clutching the pages of room charges along with the returned checks. The sounds he heard were animalistic and were met with his bellboys' terrorized shrieks. The head bellman took a step forward and craned his neck to gaze into the left bedroom. The white satin bedspread bloomed blood. When he made his hasty retreat past the manager, he cried, "Run! So much blood!"

The manager's brow creased and with noble luster in his eyes, he set his jaw and headed into the breach. The carnage before him paled his blood and choked his breath. Ragdolls of men were tossed and strewn around the room, their life's blood in puddles beneath them. With a gulp of air, he drew attention to himself, and the two fiends feeding on a single bellboy of tender years dropped their prey in unison. Samuel wiped his blood-stained lips with the back of his arm and leered. Jonas shook his head and a growl rumbled from his chest. As they advanced toward the older man, he clutched his chest and seized. He was dead before he hit the floor.

Samuel pried the papers out of the dead man's hands. "Our checks bounced!"

Jonas rolled the man on his back with his foot. He bent close, scrutinizing the canceled checks. "Impossible."

Samuel prowled like a caged tiger. "What has our dear sister been spending money on?" He kicked away the bodies and moved into the shower. Red trails sluiced down his toned body. "We need to, as they say, vamoose! We're no longer welcome."

Jonas sniffed. "I can't imagine why we'd stay if we're not wanted." He stepped into the other end of the shower and cleaned off the remnants of his hasty snack. "If we're insolvent, where can we go?" He dried off and threw clothes together into his valise. "I imagine we should only take one bag. They're going to be after us."

Samuel frowned. "If they'd only called, they wouldn't have upset us." He gestured to the seven dead men. "This is their fault. It was their lack of gentility." He picked up his Homberg and dropped it on his shaved head. "Going to the ship would be inconvenient, but the perimeter tunnels would be available."

"If it's good enough for our liquor, it's good enough for me." They strode out of the bungalow as if heading out for a gentlemen's walk. Once they were hidden in the thick palms, at vampire speed, unseen by mortals, they jumped the fence and bolted to safer ground.

13

The salt air stung Venus's vampire sensibilities and a new moon covered the dirty business of the Moreau's bootlegging. Rick and Matt, dressed as night fishermen, rowed the little skiff, skirting the coastline. They dropped Venus and Luna onto the rocky beach south of the series of caves the Moreaus used as liquor warehouses. Their police informant identified the entry password of a month ago to be 'dunes', and this was the password Venus would give when they were stopped at the mouth of the cave.

Two toughs in black stood in the dark arch. "Ladies, this ain't no dance club. Keep walking."

Venus took an assessing sniff. Mortals with guns, probably with silver bullets. She lowered her lashes demurely. "Dunes."

When they made no response, she added, "We're here to see Samuel and Jonas."

"Dunes?" He glanced questioningly at his cohort. "They're a little late, wouldn't you say?"

His partner bit his unlit cigar and shrugged. "I'll see to it." He turned, dejectedly, and disappeared into the cave.

Luna made exaggerated gestures to keep her hairstyle intact. "Are you going to keep us standing in this breeze? Jonas likes his dolls to be spiffy."

The hapless guard motioned. "Over there, out of the wind." It wasn't much closer, but they moved to stand along the cliff wall.

Samuel Moreau stepped into the starlight, and Venus was immediately struck by his arresting good looks. Well, the Moreaus were always beautiful people with dark hearts. "I have not called you here. You're trespassing." He stood with powerful arms folded over a broad chest. His sneer was evident, highlighted by the dim starlight playing on the planes of his dark skin.

"I gave the only password Veronique shared." Hands on hips, Venus challenged him. "Your sister told me to find you if I ever needed help."

Luna posed with her finger tapping her chin. "I suppose that's why Ronnie left them behind. What good are they?"

Jonas bolted from the dark. "Your words are inflammatory. What is your business here?"

Venus shook her head. "Do I have mush-mouth? I need *your* help."

"How do you know our sister?" Samuel sniffed.

"When she owned the Sunset Grande, I often supplied the shills she used to draw in mortals." The brothers moved closer to Venus. *Can they scent veracity?* Her iron gaze held Samuel's. "The night she was staked, I was there. I saw how she was railroaded. She graciously left my name out of it, but there are those in the vampire family who know of our association."

Samuel sneered. "We are not one big happy family. Why are you here?"

"Because of my alliance with the Moreaus, I've been persecuted. Now, I'm without a home or business, but I have something that will benefit us all."

Jonas gave a bored look. "That's a sad tale. What do you want with us?"

Luna shook her blonde curls. "Civility? Consideration?" She turned to Venus. "How could a doll like Ronnie have brothers like them?"

Venus turned away. "Why are we beating our gums? We'll head for Mexico and contact Ronnie from there. She'll come through."

"What do you think she'll say when we tell her these two don't know from nothin'?" Luna hooked her arm around Venus's waist and stepped toward the shore.

Strong hands clamped their shoulders and Samuel's words moved on his cool breath. "Stay. You're right, the ordeal of the past few weeks has made us suspicious. Excuse our lack of compassion. We are all in this, evidently."

Jonas bowed formally. "Please, won't you join us for some refreshment? We'll talk like the civilized creatures we are."

****

97

Matt realized with some surprise how much he missed the ocean in the weeks since he became a vampire. Even though he painted sunsets on the beach, it actually never occurred to him how peaceful the ocean was at night. The skiff rocked in the surf, and the two vampires kept a sharp eye out for Venus and Luna's return. It was over thirty minutes since the women followed the Moreaus into the cave.

"Pops, what's this dagger thing you're baiting them with?" Matt asked.

"When I was mortal, I was the Duke of Erne in Ireland. Our family had an ancestral dirk…" Matt's brows rose. "It's a close-quarters weapon. You see them hanging at men's waists in Holbein portraits."

"Oh."

"Somehow, the ridiculous rumor got started that my family's dirk was cursed and was the only weapon that could kill me."

Matt leaned back in the boat and chuckled. "Boy, you must really be somebody for a rumor like that. I could tell right off you were no ordinary guy."

Rick furrowed his brows. "I am a vampire."

Matt scratched at his jaw. "Emm… It's more than that, though. You've got old-world polish. I could read it off the refugees in the Paris train stations. They might have been broken, but manners and breeding couldn't be taken from them. The Huns could see it too, and they harassed them more than the other classes."

Rick sat ramrod straight. "Are you implying I am a snob?"

"Not exactly, but you're not living with the chickens."

"If I lived with chickens, you'd be right there with me."

Matt chuckled. "See, the difference is, I've lived with chickens before." He shrugged. "So, when did this dagger thing start?"

Rick's laughter reached his eyes. "Oh, I want to say, in the 1730s. I stopped over in Haiti on my way to the Colonies. There was a Moreau pirate ship, captained by one of their savage cousins. Her crew was mixed, mortals and vampires. She was light of treasure, and they were moving her from Port Au Prince to Havana. The problem was half the mortals on board had the pox."

"Smallpox?" Matt grimaced.

Rick nodded. "I couldn't let her sail into Cuba, with such a deadly plague. Simon Moreau refused to listen to reason, so I killed them."

Matt chuckled and leaned toward Rick. "On the level?"

"It wasn't hard. The mortal crew was infected. The vampires fed off their infected shipmates. It was easy pickens'. I burned the ship and sank her, but there was one little fella, a deck boy, who wasn't infected. I sent him off with a pound note and he must have started the rumor."

"You're just like Billy the Kid."

Rick snorted. "Well, anyway, if they think they need the dirk to kill me, advantage to me."

"Let's just hope the ladies can sell it. Undercover work is tough. Where is this dirk?"

Rick shook his head. "I have no idea. The last I heard, my family was going to bury it, thinking it brought bad luck. But that was the end of the eighteenth century, so who knows?"

"I can't believe everything you've seen."

"Right now, I want to see Venus and Luna walk out of that cave."

✳✳✳✳

Jonas posed on the end of a barrel. "What made Veronique think this was *the* dirk?"

Venus licked her lips. "I assume, she had it authenticated. When she showed it to me, it was quite unforgettable. An engraved gold and silver blade, a gold handle encrusted with precious jewels, and on the pommel, an enormous emerald carved with the family crest."

Samuel frowned. "I've heard of the dirk, of course, it was used in the murder of my kinsman, years ago, but I've never seen it, though I understand there's a portrait that features it."

"How did Veronique come by this?" Jonas asked.

"I believe through an antiquities dealer who didn't realize it's worth."

Samuel's suspicion came to the forefront. "And why are you sharing this information with us?"

Venus clutched at her bosom. "I hate Rick Hiatt. He's destroyed me. Veronique and I were living the high life. We were raking in the dough. Then, his miserable ward, Matt Brenner, stumbled into the Sunset that night. Well, Ronnie was taken with him immediately. She turned him, and the

100

bastard bolted, and ultimately whined to Hiatt that Ronnie had made him a monster. Naturally, Hiatt used it as an excuse to accuse her of a rape turn, and just look what's happened since."

Jonas looked confused. "But you still had your business…"

Luna piped up. "Not for long. Everyone was afraid to be associated with us." She spit on the ground. "Hiatt was at our door, demanding free services almost nightly. You can't build a business that way."

"Then," Venus picked up the narrative, "only three days ago, there was a gas explosion which took down my entire home and business. The police said it was an accident. But I know better. Only that night, I told Hiatt he and his friends were no longer welcome, and my place is leveled." Samuel and Jonas exchanged looks which Venus caught with a secret smile. "Anything we can do to eliminate Hiatt will be my life's work."

Samuel strolled to a heavily strapped wooden crate. "You say Veronique buried the dirk?"

Venus nodded. "She told me she buried it in one of the tunnels under the Sunset."

"Which one? There's so many." Jonas asked, exasperated.

Venus shook her head sadly. "That I can't tell you. I hoped you communicated with Ronnie. Can't we find out from her?"

Samuel pried the lid from the crate. "Sadly, she's incommunicado for the foreseeable future."

"Oh." Venus pretended to sag and then brightened. "But you could buy the Sunset and then we could take our time searching for it. It would all be yours."

"We'll put in a bid through a broker tomorrow. I must say, Miss Aquillius, your information has proved valuable." Samuel pulled a dusty bottle from the crate. "Let's drink to the end of Richard Hiatt." He turned the label toward the group. "Brandy to celebrate our alliance?"

Venus smiled charmingly. "How lovely. Luna and I must take our leave after a toast, we're hosting a party ship now that our beautiful home is gone. We have to be there to make sure everyone gets fed."

14

Paquet buried his head in his hands. "You fellows do realize my superior officer is staked in your cellar. If we don't get a confession from the Moreaus, I am liable to have my head separated from my shoulders."

Rick laid a fatherly hand on Paquet's shoulder. "We're well aware of that, Giles."

Adam paced the room, his long legs eating up the carpet. "Line 'em up against the wall and threaten to…"

Matt threw up one hand. "Flame them?" He threw up his other hand. "Behead them?"

Adam grimaced. "I don't think I have the stomach to be a vampire."

Paquet shook his head. "That wouldn't work anyway, that's coercion. They have to give us the confession freely."

Matt negated that thought with a slice of his hand. "Never happen, but… I worked undercover long enough to know that sleight of hand or trickery can wring the truth out of the devil."

"Pray tell?" Rick probed.

"Well, these are the elements of a sting... First, make them believe the object of their keenest desire is within their grasp. Next, make them believe their lives are at stake and there is no way out. Finally, convince them confession is the only thing that will save them, and do it in a way no rational person would believe."

Rick sat in deep thought for several moments, running his thumb over his lower lip. "You know, the Haitians are a fairly superstitious lot… "

"Oh?" Matt grinned.

"Yes. Voodoo and all that… It might prove useful…"

Adam nodded slowly and when he looked up his eyes were brilliant with intensity. "Have you heard of this invention by a fellow in England named Hughes? He has a device called a micro-fone…"

****

Matt exited the bank building, replacing his fedora to shield his eyes. "When does this extreme allergy to sunlight stop? You don't even flinch." He regarded Rick in his Fedora and sunglasses as they hurried to the car.

"I'm sorry to have to drag you out early, banker's hours are just that. Still, this was a satisfying meeting. We break ground in October. The days will be shorter soon." Rick let Matt into the shaded back seat and situated himself in the driver's seat. "If you got more nourishment and fewer gymnastics you might be better rested."

"Horsefeathers!"

"Seriously, dear boy, tolerance to sunlight is influenced by your general state of nutrition and rest. Entertaining Luna may be relaxation, but it's not rest." Rick pulled the car into traffic and at the first stop sign, a young boy hoisted a newspaper in the air.

"Extra, extra. Murder spree continues in Beverly Hills."

Matt rolled down the window and waved a coin at the boy. "Over here." The headlines screamed 'Mad Dog Murders, Seven Slain." Traffic resumed, and Matt read. "A Beverly Hills Hotel bungalow was the site of a grisly end for seven hotel employees yesterday morning. Unnamed sources report seven bodies were delivered to the coroner's office. Six of the seven were mauled by what appeared to be wild dogs. The seventh possibly witnessed the attacks and collapsed from apoplexy."

"Well, that does nothing to keep the family discrete." Rick glanced at Matt in the rear-view mirror.

"You know damn well this has the Moreau's signature all over it." Matt folded the paper with disgust and slumped against the seat. When his arms folded over his chest, he felt the envelope he'd placed in his breast pocket before they left home. "I can only imagine what this is. Mabel gave me something from a cop who stopped by." He opened the envelope and read it aloud. "Matt, the shmoes have headed to San Francisco on the Coast Starlight; they bought round-trip tickets for two days. No idea what they're after in the Bay area, but after the bungalow incident, they're lying low." Matt groused and ripped the letter in halves over and over. "I've just caused another series of murders."

"You were a soldier and a cop for almost ten years; did you take every death personally then?"

"I didn't cause those."

"You didn't cause these, either."

"Yes, I did. If I hadn't played the avenging angel and just sold them the property, none of this would have happened."

Rick stopped behind a column of cars at another stop sign. "Applesauce. You don't know that. The Moreaus have used murder as a business tool for centuries. Maybe you were the provocation, maybe not, but sooner or later they would have done the same thing."

"Thank you for trying to lift my spirits, but don't spit in my ear and call it rain." He glanced around an unfamiliar part of town. "Where are we headed, anyway?"

"We're going to get you a smile. Ever heard of Brooksedge?"

****

Brooksedge was one-part warehouse, one-part midway and one-part fascinating characters. Rick led Matt through alleys of glass boxes, guillotines, straitjackets and magic rings. "I'm not smiling yet. Where are the scary clowns?"

"This is magic, not the circus." He hailed a figure at the end of the warehouse. "Alphonse!" A man looked up from his preoccupation with a deck of cards.

"Richard! Welcome. Pick a card." The owl of a man with dark, mesmerizing eyes held up a fan of playing cards. Rick nodded to Matt who obligingly plucked a card. Alphonse looked away. "Don't show me the card." Matt and

Rick silently identified the Queen of Hearts. Alphonse held out his hand for the card face down and deftly placed it with the deck back into the box. He held the box before Matt and commanded. "Concentrate on your card. I divine that you have a supernatural touch, so wave those magic fingers here." He pointed under the box in his hand. "Think, concentrate, the card will respond to your mental call," Matt smirked, and Rick stood back smirking harder. Within a moment Alphonse held the box up and The Queen of Hearts rose from the rest of the deck. "Is this your card?"

Matt chuckled. "Pretty good."

Alphonse bowed from the waist. "Thank you."

"Matt, meet the Amazing Alphonse of Genoa."

"As a kid, I wanted to be a magician, my Mom said it was the work of the devil."

"Sometimes those mothers are my secret followers." He motioned them toward a table and chairs. "What can I do for you, my friend?" He uncorked illegal spirits with a suspicious label and held up the bottle. "Join me?"

They sat for a drink and Rick posed a question. "I need a masterful illusion, grander than anything at Carnegie Hall." He spread out sketches.

****

Samuel and Jonas Moreau emerged from the cab just outside the entrance of the Hallidie Building. The modern skyscraper, built in 1917, flaunted the warnings of the city engineers with its twenty-story height and wall of windows. The real estate brokers who occupied the modern structure were purported to be the most

107

successful and influential in the state. Let Matt Brenner turn down an offer from them!

As the cab pulled away it backfired, and a flurry of birds startled, their wings beating furiously among the pedestrians. Jonas waved a bird away and stood frozen. Samuel turned, realizing he walked alone, and a large black swallowtail butterfly flitted casually between the brothers.

"Mon Dieu!" The brothers exclaimed in unison and stepped back from the lilting butterfly. It hesitated in midair and then bolted for the treetops.

Staring at each other, Jonas barked. "This is a curse. This can only mean bad news, that black butterfly."

Samuel shook his head. "It's gone; it flew in front of you, not me."

"So, it's only my curse?" Jonas threw up his hands.

"Yeah, my brother." Samuel brushed at his suit with the gris-gris he pulled from his pocket. "Here. Come." He stepped closer to Jonas and waved the cleansing talisman all around his shoulders and head. "Satisfied?"

Jonas sneered, "I'll be satisfied when that ungrateful whelp, Brenner, is out of our undead lives."

****

The pool water was refreshingly brisk this evening as Rick make his fortieth lap. The jumble of possibilities in his head astounded him. What would they do to protect the population if they lost out to the Moreaus? Would he survive to relocate? The best outcome would be to prevail over the Moreaus. He'd covered every contingency; the plan should work. But Rick had lived long enough to know the perfect

108

plan rarely works perfectly. He swam deeper, working his muscles harder under the water when two strong hands gripped his shoulders. Yanking him up out of the water, Matt grinned with childlike glee.

"They couldn't help themselves. I doubled the asking price and this afternoon a telegram arrived from Dewey, Cheathem, and Howe in San Francisco. They have 'investors' who wish to buy the property for cash."

"We're sure it's our marks?"

"Yeah, confirmed by Giles. They'll be heading back on the morning train. My broker is preparing the papers; we can ride over tonight and do the deal."

Rick pinched Matt's cheek. "This is sheer genius, you're getting twice the price and when they're carted off in Responder custody, the property will come back to you as part of the restitution settlement."

Matt's blue-green eyes sparkled for the first time in a month. "It does work out nicely."

"You'll be rich, dear boy." Rick slapped his back with a wet hand.

"That's not the best part." Matt chortled as he stepped out of the pool fully clothed. "The best part is, they'll be poor and in custody."

15

Rick's playroom was illuminated with dozens of stained-glass rosette windows. The jewel tone glass, artificially backlit, gave their naked flesh a warm and rosy characteristic. This enlivened perennially pale vampires, and their mortal 'dance' partners felt more 'normal'. Even two vampires in bed liked to at least *look* alive.

Luna stretched gracefully in the feather bed. Her lips were over-kissed, plump, and pink from drawing Matt's handsome scruffy face over them repeatedly.

"Do you seriously want to do this, Matthew? I'm more than thrilled to explore impact play with you, but I don't want you to feel forced."

"What do you mean impact play?"

"Well, you asked me to teach you what Rick was doing to Venus."

"So, impact play is whips?"

"Not necessarily. It can be spanking with your hand all the way up to a cat o' nine tails. Basically, one partner is struck by another for the sexual satisfaction of one or both. The key word is consensual, my sweet." Her lashes fluttered as his cooling body covered her. The divine weight of his broad, muscled chest gave her the vapors.

So much man, so much power, so much raw, humming pleasure.

"Tell me why I'd ever enjoy that." He challenged. "I've never struck a woman, why would I want to?" Matt drew her out of the bed's cocoon to straddle his hips. Her creamy breasts hung within his lip's reach. She teased him with their sway as she concocted her reasons to entice him to use the flogger or perhaps a crop on her.

Her blonde curls cascaded forward, creating a frisson on his pecs. "My earliest erotic fantasies unfailingly portrayed me in passive roles. I didn't discover how spanking could change my life until Venus showed me. It's powerful and a bit daunting, but that was why I adored it. I feared the pain, yet I also knew the Dom or Dominatrix spanking me understood my boundaries. You always discuss that sort of thing ahead of time."

"Boundaries, permission. Is this making love or is this… commerce?"

"When a Dom administers impact, the sub has control. I'm able to stop it or dictate how hard you strike me." Luna swayed, her hips grinding against him, reawakening his hungry flesh. "You're not randomly hitting me. We use words, called safe words. They guide your strokes. I say red for stop or yellow for slow down." Luna grasped Matt's hand and played, drawing a pink fingernail over the love line in his palm. "If I say 'green' that means keep going." She suckled his index finger as his other fingers tapped lightly on her lips. He withdrew his hand from her mouth and rolled her rosy nipple. "We can use toys, too."

"Toys? Like Rick and his bullwhip? You said it would take me a while for that kind of control." Matt's tongue skirted his bottom lip as she felt his assessing gaze.

Is he going to kiss my left breast or my right breast, first?

"A whip or a flogger. I'll bet these strong hands of yours would masterfully control a lambskin flogger." She bent closer, her right breast teasing his lips and tongue as she dug behind her mountain of pillows for a short-handled flogger. His hands cupped her breasts and she giggled and sat back, gently dropping the small toy on his chest.

"What?" His chin tucked to see the black spidery item. She stretched out his arm and raised the flogger.

Their gazes met and with a raised brow she asked, "Red, yellow, green. Remember what they mean?"

"Stop, slow down, keep going."

"Good. I promise to be gentle." She ran the soft suede flogger's fifty tails up and down his forearm, with a tickling stroke. His lips curled into a boyish grin.

"Ummm." Matt's eyes closed, and his head dropped back. "Green… green…"

Her speed increased as she crossed his chest and danced the buttery suede over his nipples. They pebbled, and he thrust his hips up and back in rhythm with his sighs. "Green…"

Luna's spine tingled, feeling her power over him. She anticipated him returning the favor. Abruptly she raised the flogger straight above his chest and shimmied back from his hips. The thongs trailed from this throat to his thatch of pubic hair and the uptick of speed made him purr. "You like?" Her body swayed back and forth, the thongs and her hips alternating their pressure on his sex and his chest.

His rumbles deepened. "You are making me hornier than I have ever been, how is it possible, you vixen?"

"This type of impact gets us started. It's not pain, its titillation. If I strike with a heavier hand it stimulates a whole new sensation. I can push you to the point of stinging and it would get your motor going, almost like a mortal's adrenaline. It's one of the friendlier ways for vampires to feel alive."

Luna watched a myriad of emotions wash over Matt's face. "Alive? Do it."

Luna moved off him and the bed. She held out the flogger, pointing to a St. Andrew's cross. "There, stand to face the cross."

Matt looked around the room with a naughty grin. Delight in the forbidden, evident in his haste.

"If I were a Domme, I'd tell you to assume the position, but, for right now, hold on to the ropes." She was overcome by the play of muscles across his back when he stood obediently, arms lifted. What a divine playground for her to arouse. His slim hips curved downward enticingly to firm buttocks and muscular thighs.

Oh, I should have told him to face me, so I could see that proud cock of his stiffen at my first strike.

"Ready?"

"Push me."

Luna was not about to bring pain, not yet. Let him experience for himself the pleasure principle of impact play. Warming up her wrist, she whipped the flogger out of Matt's field of vision. At the sound of the rapid swishing, he jumped. She gave a low, evil chuckle. Without breaking her rhythm, she raised her arm and swept a figure eight of nimble strokes back and forth over his buttocks.

****

His exclamation rode a throaty growl. "Fu…, that's good!" Could this be a new way to cope with his unwanted undead nature? "Again… harder…"

"Green?"

"The greenest…"

She started at his neck and Matt could feel the bite of each tassel as she struck with greater energy, moving methodically down his back. His cock throbbed with the rhythm of her strikes. Each percussion swelled him thicker and harder.

"Greener."

There was dead silence. No movement in the room, save for Matt's excited panting.

"What, where did you go? He hung in suspended anticipation. He looked over his shoulder and jumped. Luna was within centimeters of his body, and he could feel her hunger as she dropped the flogger and began drawing her long, sharp nails down the sides of his thighs.

It was a different sensation. Gone was the soft suede, replaced by pointed fingernails. She alternated the brisk downward movement with the delicate pads of her fingertips. The unexpected mixture of prickly and delicate didn't prepare him when she grabbed his hips and spun him to face her. Dropping to her knees, she smiled up at him and swallowed him whole.

His hips bucked, filling her throat. Her delicate hands betrayed their soft appearance when she grasped him fiercely and he felt the bite of all ten fingernails in his glutes. His hips began a slow roll that escalated in force and speed. Fire rose from his root, and he wanted to scream when Luna fell back on her heels. Her lips gleamed wet, her expression wanton. She danced her fingertip over her breasts and pebbled her nipples, flaunting her charms.

"Don't stop! What the hell are you doing to me?"

"Assume the position." Her voice was steely.

Matt groaned, but the next sensation had his blood singing. The sting plucked a primal wire within his groin. He prayed to hear the sound of whatever she was using to initiate the sacred stinging. Suddenly physical pain replaced the roar of the mental torment that swept over him the moment he awoke as a vampire. His mind flew free, and he staggered into the cross, throwing up his hands to hold on for more.

"Matt… do you need me to stop?"

His voice was guttural. "No, don't stop. Let me come. Please."

Luna moved to the other side of the cross and caught his gaze. "What do you want, Matt?"

"I want to fuck you. I want you to fuck me. I just want to come."

"I want you to come." Luna pranced over to the foot of the four-poster bed and leaned over the footboard. With each of her steps, his gaze burned over her supple curves. She was dimpled at the top of her buttocks. How had he missed that? He wanted to kiss those dimples and bite her rounded cheeks. His hands spread on her hips, and he playfully pinned her.

"I can scent your arousal. You want to come, too." He growled, bent over her, nuzzling her neck as his thick cock split her sex. With a shuddering thrust, he was hilt deep and his strokes commenced. She met his urgency, her hips arching to ride the pleasing curve of his steely length. He caught both her breasts eagerly and his fangs dropped. His hoarse cry muffled into a pillowy breast as he bit, long ivory fangs drawing her dark red blood. Luna threw her forearm into her mouth and together they collapsed in completion.

They crawled back into the nest of pillows and spooned. Matt drew back her blond curls and kissed her ear. "I get it."

16

Their group of five pulled up at the Brooksedge warehouse that evening. Adam, Alphonse, and his theatrical construction crew had the skeleton of the trick-chamber ready for inspection.

Adam greeted them effusively. "You're gonna love this. I can't believe how well it works."

Rick offered a spirited grin. "Lead on, dear fellow. We're keen to see the full effects." In the warehouse, Alphonse stood in the center of a box-like concrete shell balanced on a fulcrum. "Rick, we're just finishing the mud stucco, have a look."

"Well done, Alphonse looks like the tunnels to me."

Alphonse nodded. "It will even look more so once we load the rubble. What sort of features would you like, a rickety table and chairs? I'm thinking a torch holder we can rig to look as if the lack of oxygen is reducing the flame.

Matt admired the artistry. "But we don't need oxygen, do we?" He held his breath.

Rick tapped him playfully on the back of the head. "Of course, we don't. But the illusion of the torches being extinguished adds to the threat once the 'earthquake' begins."

Adam rubbed his palms together gleefully. "Listen to this." He nodded, and a voice seemed to call from a long distance. It was a woman's voice, but reedy and faint. "Help me, someone, please, help me."

Beside Rick, Venus shuddered. "That's horrible, what is that?"

Adam applauded. "Folks, meet Iris, Alphonse's mate and assistant in his magic act."

The disembodied voice exclaimed. "I did radio in New York City."

Venus applauded too. "You're giving me the heebie-jeebies."

Adam practically danced in excitement. "You ain't heard nothin' yet." They could see a young girl of about nine years wearing sausage curls, sitting among wooden crates, an odd metal contraption in front of her.

"Momma, momma, where are you?" It was her voice, but distorted and haunting. "Momma, you didn't come home last night."

Luna shivered. Matt folded his arms over his chest and looked around. "If that doesn't get to you, nothing will."

Alphonse laughed. "She's the best little carny actress we've ever had. That's enough, Ellie. You're scaring these good people."

Laughter echoed. Over the mechanical device, it was somehow demonic. Alphonse turned to Rick. "You have the items to be planted?"

Rick produced a prop dagger with a green stone set in the handle, along with some genuine pieces of gold, an earring, a coin, a chalice. "Seeding these among the rubble should work nicely."

Iris joined them, weighing the dagger in one hand. "It feels real."

Rick opened a small notebook. "Are we a go for eleven fifteen tomorrow night at the Sunset?"

Alphonse nodded. "We'll be ready, but how will you get them here unconscious?"

Rick grinned. "In my travels, I've discovered the fruit of a few flowers that will cause unconsciousness, even in vampires. We won't have long. Twenty minutes at the most to get them from the tunnel, to here."

Matt analyzed the route. "That time of night, shouldn't be a problem."

Rick stuck out a hand to Alphonse. "I'll owe you, my friend. Consider your next world tour financed."

****

Adam was at the wheel as Rick, Matt and Giles sat back to discuss the desired outcome of their strategy. Matt turned to Rick in the back seat. "You realize the best-planned sting can unravel at a moment's notice."

121

"That's why I carry stakes and machetes, but I'd rather do this legally." He turned to Giles "I know you can't trust fellow Responders until you can prove LaTour is complicit with the Moreaus. Will family members from the Los Angeles Police suffice as witnesses?"

"Sworn statements will do nicely."

Rick nodded and bit his lower lip. "Then it's all on the acting ability of our women."

****

Venus and Luna were easily the most fashionable and beautiful women waiting on the platform. As the train rolled to a stop, the eager vampires pushed ahead of other passengers to be the first off. Venus nudged Luna. "Look how those two fools rush into our clutches." The ladies buried laughter as the men elbowed through the waiting crowd and stood before them.

Samuel doffed his hat. "I believe, mon Cheri, you two are the most stunning women in California."

Not to be outdone, Jonas caught each of their delicate hands and pressed cool lips in a kiss. "Ladies, let our evening begin. We've had a quartet of O positive beauties delivered to the Sunset Grande, their destiny awaits, let's not be tardy."

Venus hid her unease as she led the way to their car. "Luna and I have already dined and unless you're famished, our discovery should satisfy your hunger even more than blood."

"You intrigue me, my dear." Samuel acknowledged. "Since the Sunset Grande is back in the family, let us make haste."

122

Venus and Luna exchanged surreptitious glances, knowing the four abducted mortals would be safely returned to their homes.

****

The property's electricity was cut off and Jonas grumbled about having to adjust his vampire senses to the kitchen's darkness. "No power! What a rube. Brenner must consider himself a comedian."

Samuel caught Venus's elbow. "Come along, show us what you found."

Venus checked her pockets for the two flasks they would 'share' with the brothers and stepped confidently down the stairs into the cellar. Luna followed behind with Jonas. "This will change the balance of power, forever."

"Every successful man needs a woman by his side." Jonas crowed as he pulled Luna closer.

Luna looked askance and murmured. "I'll always be behind you, pushing." They paused at the entrance to a tunnel and Venus lit a torch and led the way down a steep incline. Vermin skittered away as they pushed deeper into the darkness. The walls wept with dank humidity, stained by years of torch-bearing bootleggers. After yards of inky darkness, the torch illuminated a dilapidated table and chairs and glimmers of gold.

Samuel fingered a fine filigreed earring. "In all this time, why wasn't this discovered before?"

Venus pressed her back against the wall. "There never was a time when Ronnie needed the dirk. You don't use a weapon until you need the weapon. Why should she have tipped her hand to Hiatt?"

123

Jonas nodded. "A secret weapon must be kept a secret."

"But now that we need it." Venus gestured toward the darkness. "Let's celebrate!" She brought out the flasks and handed one to each of the men. The ladies dipped into their purses for theirs. Luna turned the chair around and straddled it, catching the men's gazes. She raised her flask. "A wise man gets more use from his enemies than a fool from his friends."

The men drank down their entire flasks and Venus's eyes glittered in the torchlight. "Gentlemen, do you see the undoing of your enemy?" She held the torch above what appeared to be a glimmer of emerald peeking out of a partially disassembled brick wall.

Samuel staggered toward the treasure, followed by Jonas. "Is that …" he and his brother crashed to the floor.

Venus looked down. "Party pooper."

****

Adam watched as, at vamp speed, Matt and Rick scooped up the comatose brothers and dumped them into the back of his waiting truck. Rick checked his cuffs and collar and started to walk away. Matt threw up a hand. "This is where it could fall apart, we need to escort our guests, to ensure the connection." Matt leapt into the truck bed and waved Rick to follow him.

Venus and Luna were already well ahead of Adam. Midnight in 1922 Los Angeles, should have been a clear path. Once they left the tight rows of businesses, buildings became sparse. Adam floored the gas and picked up the pace. They were shrouded in darkness, only the headlights cutting

124

a few feet ahead of them. One second the road was clear, and the next a black gelding, pulling a buggy, reared in front of the truck. Adam broke hard and steered away from the horse. The horse escaped, but the truck tipped on its side into the marshy ruts. Matt and Rick rolled out of the truck bed assessing the damages.

Rick shook his head. "Adam, you okay?"

Adam climbed out and dusted himself off. "Sorry gents, I'm doing better than the truck."

"If time wasn't an issue, Matt and I could tip this back, but we're mired here, and it would be quicker for us to throw them over our shoulders and run the mile."

Adam waved and walked the few yards to the frightened horse. "I'll catch up."

****

Matt groused as he shouldered Jonas in a fireman's carry. "I hated track and field." Rick gave him a sardonic glance. "There's a reason I swim every day."

"Yeah, yeah, but your suit is shot."

"A new one is coming out of the proceeds of your building sale."

"Priorities, Pops, priorities."

"Put on some speed, dear boy, or these two will wake before we get them in the box."

Just as they made it through the warehouse doors, the two Haitian vampires began to stir. With an extraordinary leap, Matt and Rick were in the box, the Moreau brothers tossed like ragdolls next to Luna and Venus who were appropriately mussed and dirtied to fulfill their roles.

125

The doors closed with a metal thud and darkness enveloped the fake tunnel. Alphonse and his team began to rock the trick-room on its fulcrum, simulating earthquake aftershocks. A micro-fone and the speaker were hidden among the rubble.

Samuel stumbled to his feet, counterbalancing on the rocking floor. "Mon Dieu! What is happening?"

Venus stayed low. "It's an earthquake. I was worried when the ceiling fell that you were crushed."

Samuel fought his way to the rickety table and held on, watching dust and debris float from the ceiling and walls. The torch flickered dimly as if starved for oxygen. "Jonas, where are you?" The chair on its side moved and Jonas struggled from under it. On his knees, he blinked and looked around.

"Are we alive? That black butterfly, it damned us."

Luna leaned against the momentarily stable wall and cried. "We survive for now but look around you. The tunnel is collapsing, we'll be crushed, and no one will know to search for us."

Matt silently signaled for more shaking and the room swayed ominously.

Venus collapsed to the floor, thrown by the violent motion. "I had a vision…" She rose from her belly to her elbows.

Luna crawled toward her. "No, not another vision, you know what happened the last time…"

Venus wiped the dust from her face. "Yes, our home was destroyed."

Samuel scoffed. "I do not believe in visions."

Jonas pushed at his brother's shoulder. "Remember the butterfly. Believe the signs, my brother."

Venus raised a brow to Luna. "I saw them… the restless dead. I saw… the child…"

Overhead the thready, disembodied voice began, faint but growing steadily more strident. "Mommy, mommy, you didn't come home and… the lady came for me." Luna gasped dramatically. "Mommy, I'm alone, she's hungry, Mommy."

Jonas hunkered down to the floor. "What is that?"

Venus nodded. "It's one of the dead victims, they haunt these grounds."

A motherly voice responded. "Oh, sweetie, I wanted to come home, but I'm held, bound by my death at the hands of these devils." The four vampires quivered as the crying began. The floor heaved, and the odor of hot sulfur erupted from the cracks. They scampered back from the opening crevice.

Venus shook her head violently and pointed at Samuel. "You brought this on us. Your family has damned this ground."

Luna struggled across the floor to embrace Venus. "My sister, we have sinned together. We have brought some of this on ourselves. Only confession can save the sinner." They wept with their heads together.

Samuel rose on unsteady legs and cursed. "I am unbowed in your face!" The 'tunnel' shook side to side, back and forth, sending all of them to the floor. "I am the master of my own fate! By my Papa's power, I will prevail."

Alphonse bent to the micro-fone and delivered a demonic chortle that became more sinister in its transmission as it echoed within the shaking prison. Luna drew herself against the wall.

Venus prostrated herself. "You must be mad to exalt yourself above Satan! I confess, Lucifer, you bought my soul. In exchange for comfort and pleasure, I led men and women astray by the whip and the pillow."

Alphonse's demonic voice raised the hair on their arms. "Only when you pledge to me with your sins, will I allow you the freedom to walk the earth. Confess your transgressions to buy your undead lives."

Jonas cowered in a fetal position. "When I was twelve, I stole a horse from the stable. I gave rides for candy…"

Samuel smacked at his brother. "Shut up, you fool. The devil is not concerned with children's petty sins. The devil requires formidable depravity."

Jonas jerked away. "Like eating the bellboys?"

"No one cares about mortals. They're food."

"Then we could buy our undead lives with confessing the fires. We burned vampires in those fires."

Samuel slapped him across the face. "Shut up, boy."

Venus pointed a shaking finger, as she charged the brothers. "*You* burned my house, my business!"

Samuel backhanded her out of the way. "Your clients were collateral damage. You gave comfort to Hiatt and his fledgling. You needed to pay."

"Other vampires did not have to pay my debts." She spat at his feet.

Samuel ranted. "Los Angeles vampires will learn respect for the Moreaus, or we will torch the city and salt the earth."

"You confess you've killed and maimed your own kind?" Venus accused.

"Yes." His chest inflated with pride. "I have powerful friends throughout the vampire family." He caught her chin and raised a brow. "I have no need of your insipid atonement."

Using her own vampire strength, Venus broke away from him. "Actually, I think you do."

Doors flew open, lights glared on. Behind the blinding illumination, eight vampires, some with flamethrowers, some with stakes and silver manacles advanced through the blinding light to subdue and arrest the bewildered brothers. As the blue-clad police stepped out of the glare into the men's personal space, the wrestling began. Venus and Luna bolted and were pulled to safety by Rick as Matt flew into the fray. Slugging through the tangle of arms and legs, Matt caught the stake Giles tossed, and pinned Samuel against the wall.

"If it consumes my eternity, I will take down every one of the Moreaus." Fury glittered in Matt's hot gaze as Samuel glared back. Matt pulled back the stake and plunged it into Samuel's heart.

The room was suddenly still. Matt turned to survey the staged cataclysm. His hands shook as he drew in a deep breath, raised his fist, and bellowed his wrath.

****

The police lowered the staked and paralyzed brothers into individual silver lined caskets for delivery to the vampire criminal justice system. Alphonse's crew struck the set. By the time Giles had the signed statements of the eight vampire cops, the Brooksedge warehouse resembled the magic shop it was.

17

The celebration wound down as the moon began its descent toward the horizon. Giles and Rick were at the train depot delivering a subdued LaTour to a cadre of New Orleans Responders. Luna and Venus toasted each other for their performances in a starring role. Matt and Adam sat in large Adirondack chairs in the tranquility of the walled garden, watching the ladies as they danced along the path kissing and giggling.

Adam sensed the strain radiating from Matt even though his shirt collar was off, and his tie discarded. He studied the fledgling vampire, taking in the tense set of his jaw. Matt was no less edgy when he asked, "You've done this BDSM thing for a while, Adam?"

"Yes," Adam confirmed and moved his crystal glass from hand to hand, as he watched the ladies canoodling. He was unsure of Matt's mood.

Matt leaned straight back, with a thousand-yard stare towards the stars. His long legs stretched out, crossed at the ankles, though he was anything but relaxed. He held the half empty decanter of single malt and his full glass. "You know how to use a whip. Do you use a bullwhip like Rick?"

"I do use a whip, but not a bullwhip. I prefer a buggy whip." There was a protracted silence and Adam probed. "You writing a book?"

Matt barked out a laugh. "Have you ever used it… on a man?"

Adam swung around to scrutinize Matt. "Matt, I like women."

"Yeah, I love women. So, the whipping thing is like the screwing thing?"

Adam leaned forward, his hands folded between his knees. "Let me catch up here… What are you asking, Matt?"

"Luna used a crop on me, but she doesn't have the strength… You're a big guy and I thought maybe you could put your arm into it."

"You're asking for pain."

"I guess so, yes."

"But you don't come across as a masochist. You get a sexual thrill from the pain?"

Matt recoiled. Sitting up and hunching over, he poured another glass of scotch. "God, no. Who would do that?" He swallowed the drink.

"A masochist."

Matt chuckled. "I'm definitely not a masochist. But… after a few lashes of the crop, the din in my soul quieted and as she laid my back open, as I bled, it silenced altogether. It was the first time since I was turned, I had peace."

Adam's face filled with concern. "She split your skin?"

Matt nodded glumly. "Don't look so horrified. Vampires heal incredibly fast. There's not a mark on me."

Adam looked away from Matt's driven expression. Then he turned to face his new friend. "And you crave it."

Matt sat back again and balanced his glass on his knee. "We were busy with the Moreaus and that kept me distracted. Now that's over. Yes, I crave it. Will you do that for me?"

"If I did, I'd be feeding a very unhealthy part of you."

"I'm undead, you can't kill me." Matt protested.

Adam shook his head. "No, Matt. I'm not going to help you deal with your emotional pain that way." He hesitated and then continued. "There was a time in my life, about a hundred years ago when I was cast of my home. Everything I'd known for eight hundred years was taken from me." Matt dropped his glass on the patio, ignoring the shattering crystal. Adam went on. "I felt robbed. I was thrown out of my element with no one to befriend me."

"You're not a vampire." Matt's brows knitted. "What are you?"

Adam chuckled. "Not all supernatural beings are vampires. I'm a dragon shifter."

Matt looked at the decanter on the table next to him and back at Adam. "A dragon… shifter…" His laughter doubled him over and he came back up, one hand over his mouth begging forgiveness. "I… I don't mean to dismiss your curse. Who did that to you?" Suddenly, Matt was empathetic.

Adam laughed, now. "You'd have to blame my parents, I was born that way. But, exile, that was different. Most of us live our few thousand years and die within the dragon community."

"Is that in a castle? In Europe?"

Adam felt Matt's confusion. "The point I'm making is, I understand what it is to be separated from your sense of self. Like so many searchers, I've been exploring the new science of psychology. I'm beginning to understand that regardless of our nature, undead, supernatural, what have you, we all have to deal with pain. It's important to find a healthy way to do that."

Rick stepped out of the shadows. "I'm sorry, I wasn't intentionally eavesdropping. I just got home and came out to have a drink with you when I heard your conversation. I thought I should give you a moment to finish."

Matt stared at his wringing hands. "I don't mean to sound ungrateful, Rick. I've never lived like this." He gestured to the estate and his clothes. "Veronique made me a monster, and I don't know how to live as a monster."

"Dear boy, I can hear your pain." Rick crossed the patio and sat in front of Matt. He put his hand on Matt's wringing hands, calming the motion. "I want you to consider, there are many people here who love you." Matt raised a tearful gaze. "You're not a monster. Veronique took your life; she didn't take your heart."

Matt hung his head. "She took my soul." His voice was thick with emotion.

Rick and Adam exchanged sad glances. "Your soul is right where it should be, in your heart. I watched you today. You were an avenging angel. No monster could do what you did."

"The others who were turned like me, did they make anything of themselves?"

Rick was silent a long moment. "Many didn't. Many were put down in their first week. Some took their own lives incredibly early. But, Matt, you've already beaten the odds. I can't tell you how to spend your nights, but I believe there is meaning in doing good."

Matt scoffed. "As a vampire?" He ran both hands through his hair and sat back flustered.

Rick nodded. "Dear boy, the undead are on the cusp of becoming something big in this town. We've already set the wheels in motion for an industry to feed the growing vampire population. Can you imagine a world in which most vampires no longer kill to feed? Ninety to a hundred years from now, mortals won't even realize who we are, standing in a crowd next to them. We need to keep it that way."

"It seems a worthy ambition to use your superhuman abilities to help both worlds," Adam observed.

Rick's caramel eyes warmed. "Once vampires no longer kill to eat, we'll still need a code of behavior to maintain our secrets. Whether you believe it is to protect the weaker mortals or secure the veil between our worlds, secrets must be kept. You could be a part of that. It's better than laying open your flesh."

There was a silent beat between the three men. "You were a major part of closing down the Moreaus. You recruited vampire family members on the police force to end a bloody chapter in this city. Giles and I had a long discussion about bringing the Responders into California. We vampires need to stick together. We need you on our side. It's your side now."

Matt sat up and drew in a deep but unnecessary breath. Rick nodded. "Will you commit to us for a year?"

Adam offered. "A year is nothing to immortals. Twelve months will fly."

Matt's face rested in his hands for a moment and then he looked up to his friends. "Because of what you've done for me, yes, I will commit to a year." He heaved a heavy sigh.

Rick settled back and withdrew his leather cigar holder. "Let's smoke on it." He handed his cutter and a cigar to Adam. "Can you light that without a match, Sparky?"

Adam's blonde brow rose, and his lips curled into a grin. "I *could*."

Rick winked and shook a finger at Adam. "I knew you weren't mortal."

18

In a year, Matt's undead life dramatically changed. Where initially he was adrift without his career as a Los Angeles detective, now his 'night job' was as the Lieutenant Commissioner of Responders for the state of California and liaison with the local undead on the police force. Within the past twelve months, ten seasoned vampires of no less than fifty years were recruited to cover the Golden State. Giles Paquet relocated from New Orleans to assume the position of Commissioner of Responders.

****

Rick hastened Matt down the long crimson leather hallway in the newly constructed Gaoler's office wing. "It was just delivered; I'll let you personalize it."

Matt shot him a quizzical look. "Personalize what? What is it?"

Rick opened the heavy mahogany door and flipped on the lights. A massive partner's desk sat in the middle of a daunting office worthy of Wall Street. "Our desks. Of course, you have your own private office above stairs, but when we want to intimidate troublemakers we will look as formidable as we are."

Matt whistled at the shining wood surface. Rick's side already sported a fancy leather blotter, three telephones and a gold art deco pen and ink set.

"Do I get a telephone, too?"

Rick picked up the red phone and plopped it on Matt's side. "Since you're 'physical plant and security', you get the trouble line."

Matt sifted through the open mail in a leather tray. "I couldn't be happier, I sold the Sunset Grande to a developer who is dividing it into luxury apartments."

Rick smirked, "If those walls could talk, let's hope the place isn't really haunted."

Matt's brow rose, and a smile spread across his handsome face. "With my proceeds I funded a new women and children's home." Matt folded the real estate papers and filed them in a drawer. "I see Jonas and Samuel Moreau were sentenced to be 'detained for no less than fifty years'."

Rick sat up and with both hands flat on the desk, he leaned toward Matt. "They knowingly rejected the kinship of *the family*. The Vampire High Council believes support of the kinship is paramount to responsible survival. Ferals are put down because once they hit a certain point, their depravity is no longer treatable; their elimination is a mercy killing. But those who aren't feral, who know the law and deliberately violate it, well, let's just say, their punishment is unpleasant."

Matt's expression grew somber. "What do you mean by unpleasant? What happens to them?"

Rick's brow rose wickedly. "Don't worry; it's not in your code to behave that way. But what happens to the worst of them is flaming or beheading. Someone with multiple previous charges might be held in silver manacles. They're fully aware of their circumstances and how little they're fed." Matt winced and rubbed his wrists. "It gives them all the time in the world to repent their transgressions or at least vow to sin no more."

Matt was subdued. "What's a first offense punishment?"

Rick's expression lightened with a shrug. "Staking. They can see and hear but can't move a muscle. It's very boring."

"Where are they housed? Do we have a San Quentin?"

"Oh, dear boy, you almost guessed. Actually, there's a god-forsaken barge near the Galapagos Islands. Being that close to the Equator, it is a veritable oven. A ship delivers the criminals and leaves them. In their depleted condition, they could never escape. I understand the guards rotate every two weeks. No one is stationed there more than once a year. That's how atrocious their circumstances are."

"I get the punishment, but if vamp psychopaths are really human psychopaths who've been turned, then nothing completely deters them."

"True, that's where the flaming and beheading comes in. We do want to give them the one in a million chance to reform." Rick sat back and planted both feet on his desktop. He chuckled. "I'll wager it's put the fear of the law into Veronique and Papa Moreau. They're giving the United States and Europe a wide berth."

Matt sat in his chair and played with the settings, raising, and lowering it to find the best height. "It serves notice to petty vampire criminals; their crimes are a liability to the vampire community, and we won't tolerate them in California."

Rick put both hands behind his head and smiled. "Things should become peaceful and prosperous among our vampire family in very short order."

Matt rolled the chair into work mode and sorted accounting sheets. "Your idea of exchanging blood for sex is going to be very popular if we judge by the projections of this month's reservations."

Rick grinned proudly. "Already there has been a dramatic decrease in mortal deaths at the hands of vampires. Unfortunately, there will always be feeding accidents."

Matt's jubilation wilted, and he folded his hands on the desk, his expression somber. "Yes, there will always be feeding accidents. But accidents in the throes of passion are different."

Rick's demeanor flipped. "God's nightgown, you fixate on your one drug-induced accident. Whenever things are too rosy and positive, you bound right back to that night with a young lady who always skated the thin edge of peril." They were both silent a beat and Rick pounded his fist on the desk. "You weren't the drug user…"

Matt threw up both hands. "But…"

"No buts." Rick pointed a silencing finger at his partner. "She set out to tempt vamps to draw her to the edge. You don't know how many times more experienced vamps nearly did the same thing." Matt sat muted by the news. "She was the face of innocence harboring a death wish. The night she caught you up in conversation about cop families, I should have hustled you out and set you straight. You drew the short straw."

"I heard her heart stop; I saw the light go out of her eyes. Once second, she was alive, and I was too high on her blood to stop…"

"Deny yourself the comfort of living flesh if you must. I can't argue you away from that decision. But as a vamp of four hundred years, I'll tell you it wasn't about vamp/mortal sex. It was about an inexperienced vampire, a reckless woman and the influence of her cocaine-infused blood."

Matt waved his arguments away. "You may be right, but it set me straight. No more relationships with mortal women."

Rick shook his head in exasperation. "Mortals are as fragile as spun sugar. It's the risk they take when they enter our world. I'm sorry Lilly crossed your path. Understand, she was a ticking bomb."

Matt's head dropped back, and he stared at the ceiling. "It won't happen again. No more mortal women for me."

****

Searchlights danced overhead opening night, the Saturday of Labor Day weekend, 1923. What had been hot, dry, Santa Anna winds were blown out by a lovely cool-front fostering refreshing ocean breezes over the City of Angels. The weather could not have been better to draw out the holiday crowd in their satins and

141

furs. Everyone who was anyone was invited to a night of dinner and dancing at the grand opening of The Phoenix. Those with special entrée were invited to more exotic pleasures underground at The Gaoler.

Rick and Matt were in high spirits as they inspected every square foot of the new four-story Italian Renaissance revival building. Matt admired the silk draperies in the dining room. "You really go for this ornate Italian design."

Rick's boyish smile grew wide. "One day I'll tell you all about my time in Italy. Maybe, we'll even take a cruise."

"And I'll show you Paris, the way I remember it from the war. But right now,…" Matt looked at his pocket watch. "Our guests are expected. We need to get out front."

"Aren't you the perfect host?" Rick straightened Matt's tie. He turned to the Maître D. "Elliot, assemble the staff in the foyer. We'd like a word with them." The man bowed and returned with the front staff.

Matt's gaze swept over the two score employees of The Phoenix. Waiters, busboys, cigarette, and camera girls stood tall in their formal black uniforms, perfectly groomed. Matt grinned easily at them. "Nervous?" His question was answered by murmurs. "Yeah, we are too, a little. It's a big night. We all want to be sure everyone has a good time. Happy patrons make for big tips, return customers and employment for everyone. So, forget anything else going on in your life. Your total focus tonight should be giving our guests their best experience."

****

Matt rechecked his bow tie. He and Rick stood in the foyer before the ornate gilt mirror. "I haven't eaten in over a year, why do I have butterflies?" He patted his cummerbund.

"I believe they call it opening night jitters, dear boy." Rick hooked a hand in Matt's elbow and pulled him to the portico.

****

Adam arrived in an ostentatious black Packard Twin-Six limo, driven by a stiff-necked chauffeur. Matt could barely contain his enthusiasm for greeting the developer who made the Consort Group building a reality. "Hey, Sparky, flying solo tonight?"

"Tomorrow night will be for pleasure." He nudged Matt good-naturedly. "Tonight, I'm Mr. Lachlan, real estate developer.

Rick smirked. "Wait till you see The Gaoler dressed out. You'll flip; it's a regular wet dream." Adam strode apace with Rick and Matt on each side of him and they entered the luxurious host station.

"Good evening Mr. Lachlan, my name is Elliott. I'll be your Maître D this evening. Please follow me." He carried the tasseled menus and stepped ahead to lead them to a prominent table.

Matt whispered. "Check out those chandeliers. They're the cat's meow."

Adam's gaze scanned the bandstand. "Who's the kid on stage?" He asked, nodding at a tall and lanky young man in front of the orchestra with a head of wildly curling auburn hair.

Rick grinned. "Yeah, he draws all the ladies, which makes the gentlemen happy."

143

Matt's panty-dropping smile emerged. With a sparkle in his blue-green eyes, he winked. "You know those ladies are coming to see us, gentlemen."

Rick shook his head regretfully. "If only I could carry a tune."

****

The house band played dinner music as Venus, Giles, and Luna, all resplendent, followed the Maître D to the table. The men at the table stood. Adam stooped to embrace Venus lightly. "Sugar bun, you look stunning in black velvet. I swear you put every other woman in the shade." He glanced at Luna. "Except you, Luna. You still wear your bridal glow. Is tonight your first month anniversary?" Giles caught her left hand to his lips and the sparkle of Luna's engagement ring was blinding.

"Ma petite."

Luna smiled at Adam. "Nice save, Master Adam."

Adam shrugged and assisted Venus into her chair. He whispered. "I'm looking forward to tonight."

Rick tapped his ear. "Sparky, we can hear you." Rick's brow arched in amusement.

Venus purred in her smoky voice. "Wait till you see my playroom. I have some new toys; I believe you'll enjoy."

Adam sighed. "What a pleasant surprise. I expected this evening to be all work." He glanced at Rick. "When does this shindig end?"

Rick pursed his lips. "When the last patron goes home."

****

144

Rick led their group to the double doors marked 'Private'. He unlocked them with an ornate gold key and pushed both doors open to reveal an art deco, black marble staircase. Once they were past him, he pulled the doors closed with a finite click of the lock. "Ladies and gentlemen follow me to paradise."

The highly waxed sheen of the ebony wood floor sparkled in the faux carriage lights. The crimson leather walls absorbed the sound of their footsteps. "The Gaoler isn't officially open yet; we have just a few invited guests tonight."

Rick stood with his back to another set of double doors. "There's never been anything like this public demonstration room…"

Venus hugged herself. "Who doesn't love to watch a Master Dom in his element?"

Rick's lips curled in anticipation. "Let's hope our crowd shares your curiosity." He threw open the doors and flipped on the lights. Everyone scattered to inspect the various apparatus and toys, depending on their personal predilections. The demonstration platform was raised in the center of the room with comfortable settees encircling the stage. The light sparkled off the chrome and black leather of the tools of the trade.

Giles patted the St Andrew's Cross. "A padded cross, so much comfort for the pain!"

Rick bowed. "We aim to please."

Luna examined the display of crops and whips and paddles and floggers. "Oh, my, you have some items I haven't seen since I left Paris."

Matt smirked. "That was my contribution. I have some Army friends still in Paris." His chuckle was wicked.

Adam ran his hand along the thick padding of the spanking bench. "This is a wonderful bench." He bent over it, inspecting myriad positions it accommodated for restraints. "I could do some intricate Shibari with a willing submissive on this."

"Shibari?" Giles asked. "I feel I should know this, but…"

"It's ancient Japanese rope bondage, my love." Luna gave him a playful hip bump. "I'll demonstrate for you sometime."

"Ah!" Giles nuzzled her neck, drawing heckles from the group.

Venus flashed her flirtatious ebony eyes at Adam. "And when you have them restrained, what do you do with them?"

Adam's aqua eyes sparkled. "I make them tell me their greatest desires, of course."

Her voice grew huskier. "And do you fulfill them?"

Matt interrupted by clearing his throat. "I can see you're going to enjoy your playroom, Sparky."

Adam nuzzled behind Venus's ear. "I guess you'd better show us the playrooms."

They were off on the tour again. "There are private playrooms, owned by club members," Rick explained, gesturing down the hallway. "No one uses those, except the owners. There are public playrooms rentable for the night…" He gestured down an adjoining hall and gave a cocky grin… "They contain standard equipment. But for a handsome fee, they can be kitted out."

Giles laughed. "Looking at the variety, I am keen to see what you have done in your dungeon, Rick."

Rick shrugged. "It's really rather ordinary but follow me." He led them to a door he unlocked. His ornate key flashed the green fire of an emerald as he opened the door.

Venus gasped. "My stars, Richard. You have one of everything."

Rick gave a smug smile. "You knew what I was ordering."

"I did, but I didn't know what a presentation it would make. This is BDSM heaven."

Adam folded his arms and surveyed the room through his golden eyelashes. He ran an appreciative hand over an ornately carved chair. "Who do I speak with about getting one of these for myself?"

Venus spun on her heel. "I'm the Dungeon Mistress; I can make your dreams come true… for a price."

Adam approached Venus from behind, wrapped his strong arms around her shoulders and whispered. "Then your deepest desires will be satisfied on every surface, in every position, tonight." Venus shivered in anticipation.

Rick rolled his eyes. "Again, Sparky, we can hear you." Rick tapped his ear.

Matt slipped to the door and held it open. "Now, if you want to see the other extreme, my place is over here." He pointed next door. The crowd filtered into the room, surprised to see the bottle green walls and tobacco colored leather easy chairs. Tiffany lamps in geometric patterns cast a kaleidoscope of color on the ceiling.

Adam gasped and teased. "Is this the library?" He walked to the bookshelf behind the chairs in the corner. With his hands behind his back, he perused the small Hans Elischer statuette of a nude young lady with a perky bow in her short hair. A bird perched on her finger as she cooed to it. A woven copper wire ring encircled her neck, like a collar. It contrasted with the statue's deep bronze hue. "This is interesting…"

Matt turned somber as he fingered the bronze on the red marble base. "The ring has great sentimental value, and she wears it well, doesn't she?" He slid the bronze back into the depth of the bookcase and his fingertips lingered a moment. "Did you see this first edition of The Kama Sutra? It's the 1883 translation by Sir Richard Burton."

Adam accepted the book excitedly and thumbed through the illustrations. "I was beginning to lose hope for you, with all these books. Thank the gods, they're all about sex."

Matt crooked his finger and pointed around a corner. A massive four-poster bed was covered in cognac colored silk and piled with pillows of every size. "If the way to a man's heart is through his stomach, the way to a woman's heart is through the wooing." Matt opened another door to reveal a dazzling black and white bathroom. The tub stood in the center.

Giles's brows rose. "You have a swimming pool?"

Matt sat on the edge of the exceedingly large bathtub. "Haven't you heard? Women adore bubble baths." He stroked the gold plated, dolphin-shaped faucet and then nodded to the end of the room. "If you prefer bathing of the vertical type, that shower stall is the largest in Los Angeles."

Rick ran his hands over the towel bar and stacks of fluffy washcloths. "It didn't take long for you to embrace your sybaritic side, dear boy."

"You told me to play the long game. They line up at your door for discipline, they line up at mine for the eroticism of romance."

Luna's eyes lit up. "Giles, my pet, we need to remodel our bathroom." She cuddled into her mate's embrace and pulled him to a shelf of oils and scents. "Look at these massage oils, oooh." She shivered.

Matt sighed, "Vanilla is a powerful aphrodisiac." He looked over his shoulder as he carried his first edition of Rilke's Sonnets to Orpheus to the table beside his wing chair. "For all the wealth of our accoutrements, Rick, it looks like we are on our own tonight. At the least, I have a new book."

"The night is young, my protégé." Rick caught Matt's elbow "I understand Doris and Clovis will be joining us later."

Matt stopped in his tracks. "Looking for more than a bite?"

Rick threw a brotherly arm around Matt's shoulders. "Everything in moderation. Nice and easy does it every time."

Matt shook his head, his bottom lip stubbornly set. "I need a drink. Why don't we go into the lounge to enjoy one?" Closer to the staircase, he held the etched glass, art deco door open to reveal a veritable art museum with alcohol. "I did the murals myself; the sculptures are all Josef Lorenzl. I particularly love the nude woman archer. Isn't she graceful?" He walked behind the bar and proudly swept a hand to show the genuine liquor bottles on the mirrored shelves. "All of these are imported, genuine brands. What strikes your fancy?"

Venus crowed. "You have Cassis des Peres Chartreux Liquor!" She clapped her hands like a child. "I haven't seen this since 1900."

If a vampire could blush, Matt would have. "I knew it was your favorite."

Rick shook his head. "Oh, please. You like French blackberries. That's why you bought it."

Matt brought up liquor glasses and a small decanter of A positive. "I was fond of it during the war. It still goes well with A positive." He poured glasses for each of them.

The door opened and a waiter holding a silver tray excused his interruption. "This telegram came for you, sir." He bowed to Rick.

"Thanks, Andre." Rick took the yellow envelope. "Could it be congratulations from the Council Governor?" His friends murmured their suppositions. He groaned. "It's Papa Moreau." He read aloud. "I will remember and recover. Stop. I will not forgive and forget. Stop." Rick dropped the envelope on the bar and drummed his fingers on it. "Well, that's cryptic."

Giles, who had experience with Papa Moreau, shook his head and frowned, "Cryptic from any one of the Moreaus is never positive. You must stay on guard, my friend."

Rick waved his hand dismissively. "If there's anyone who understands the long game, it's Papa Moreau."

Matt let out a gust of breath. "I say to hell with him tonight. Nothing is going to tarnish our fun."

Luna clapped her hands. "Enough gloom! Let us enjoy each other in this beautiful room."

Rick knew better than to think Moreau would forget a grudge. He knew Papa would swing the blade when he least expected it.

Giles nodded uneasy agreement and walked along the walls, admiring the murals. "Matthew, I had no idea you were such an accomplished painter. These dancing figures are... very sensual. Even with six of us here, the near life-size figures create quite an intimate atmosphere."

Matt looked up from the bar. "Thank you, Giles. It was a labor of love. One of these days I'm going to abandon everything and just paint."

Rick leaned on the bar and winked. "On a mortal cop's salary, you wouldn't have been able to plan that!"

Adam raised his glass. "It's been a good year, hasn't it, Matt?"

Emotion rose in Matt's throat, and he raised his glass. "To the glory of friendship. It's not the outstretched hand of brotherhood or the joy of companionship; it's the otherworldly reassurance that comes when you discover people believe in you and are willing to trust you with their friendship."

"Here, here!" Venus whispered.

"To friendship." Rick agreed.

The End, *or the Beginning?*

Brenner's Edicts for the Undead

- ❖ Vampires are the ultimate Doms.
- ❖ Stay out of mortal's relationships; *no good comes from intervening.*
- ❖ Never get involved with mortal females; *they break too easily.*
- ❖ Emotional relationships with mortals are difficult; *they can't detach.*
- ❖ Immortality is an illusion; *vampires can be killed.*
- ❖ The number one mannerism for appearing human; *inhale/exhale, repeat.*
- ❖ To be irresistible to donors, *hang out with your fangs out.*
- ❖ The first bite is the sweetest.
- ❖ Pale is the new tan.

Vampire's Golden Rule

It's not the bite you get, *it's the bite you give.*

Blood Rising by Amber Anthony

Drop dead gorgeous alive, Matt Brenner has never lacked for feminine attention. Undead, he's even more potent. Immortality would be stellar if only he accepted his life as a vampire. Matt and fellow vamp Richard Hiatt created a BDSM empire catering to Vampire/Doms and willing donor/subs who trade sexual ecstasy for blood. The clubs have made Matt's existence manageable, if uninspired.

Inspiration comes in the form of Catherine Temple.

Matt's made it a rule not to get emotionally involved with human women, and he sticks to it. Cat is the woman who can entice him to break all the rules. When Matt is introduced to a controversial drug that allows him a human lifetime with Cat, it's too exquisite to resist.

Powerful elements of the vampire nation are against it, and though Matt tries to protect Cat, love must be stronger than death.

Blood Rising Excerpt

They continued along the hall until they reached Cat's battered green door, and Matt wondered when they'd gutted the formerly expansive residences and replaced them with squalid studio and one-bedroom apartments.

"Well, you did a good job of that." He grinned.

She turned carefully innocent eyes up to him. "What?"

"Making sure everyone knew who I was and where to find me."

"It seemed polite."

He shook his head with another grin. "Right. So, ask me in. We still need to talk."

"Do I have to ask you in?" she whispered.

He gave her a flummoxed glance. "Uh…no, but I'm not the kind of guy to push my way into your place."

"Okay," she murmured, still cautious.

She opened the door to what might have been the smallest studio apartment he'd ever seen. It was neat, utilitarian, and stark. Matt was struck by the large open space that dominated the middle of the small room until he realized the wood paneling centered on the wall was a Murphy bed. Cat gestured him onto the loveseat and leaned against the closed door.

She gave him a direct look. "Talk."

His stare back was just as direct. "Tell me what you think you saw."

"I know I saw you turn into something…in-human."

"In-human, huh?" he pondered. "Then…what would that make me?"

"Something I don't understand. Are you…an alien?"

Matt looked aside to squelch a smile, returning a serious face to her. "You mean, like from Mexico?"

"No, I mean, like…" She bit her lip and pointed upward.

"From upstairs?"

She laughed nervously. "No, I'm pretty sure everyone in this building has to prove citizenship."

"Ah…so, farther up? Like outer space?"

"Yeah, like outer space."

"No. I'm definitely from Los Angeles."

Cat paused and pondered what that could mean. "Then, what are you? Because what I saw…"

"I'm a vampire."

"That's impossible."

"You saw it for yourself. It's not the way I would choose to introduce my nature, but shit happens."

She drew into herself again. "So, is this when you kill me?"

Matt buried a laugh. "Not tonight." And at her alarmed gasp, he added soothingly, "Not ever. I'm not ever going to kill you."

"Vampires are killers…"

"Maybe in bad B movies. Real vampires have a lot of different ways of eating, without killing. You'd be surprised."

"Oh. What's it like to be a vampire?" Her voice cracked as she pulled a pillow off the sofa and jumped back to the door. The upholstered would-be shield could do nothing to protect her. She feigned nonchalance. "Do you spend your life avoiding crosses and garlic? Is that why you're taking night classes?"

He looked at her from under his lashes. Her breath hitched. "Yeah, sunlight is a problem. It tires me out. I prefer nights."

Cat shifted fretfully and glanced toward the kitchenette wall. "May I get you a drink? I think I have some brandy left over from when I had the flu."

She nervously licked her lips, and in two steps, unearthed the barely touched bottle of Gallo's brandy from a cabinet in the miniscule kitchen. Matt held up a halting hand.

"Well, I need a drink." She reached for a glass in the dish drainer and then poured a splash. She stood expectantly, her back against the metal cabinets, and waited.

"Look, I know you have a natural curiosity about me. The thing is, I overheard your conversation with Brad when I arrived for class tonight, and I didn't think it was right to leave you alone with him, so I got involved. Are you sorry I did?" She slowly shook her head. "I'm not sorry, either. You know if I'd been human…he meant to kill me."

"You must be invincible? I mean, first Brad and then the car."

"Yeah." He frowned, rejecting her line of questioning, and returned to the issue most on his mind. "Brad's a bad guy, Cat. I want you to stay away from him."

"Not that I'm arguing that point, but do vampires also order strangers around?"

He snorted and stared at her for a beat, drawing his brows across his forehead with concern. "How the hell did you get involved with a guy who has Domination fantasies? Do you really want to be a sub?"

"A what?" she asked with genuine innocence.

"A submissive." He paused. "You don't have a clue what I'm talking about, do you?"

She shook her head. "What are 'subs'?"

Matt pursed his lips. "It's a sexual fetish. I'm guessing you don't have much experience with them."

"I'm a writer," she declared before she drained the glass. "I should learn about everything."

He looked away, ruthlessly squelching a grin. "Stay away from Brad."

"Yeah. I already figured that out." She hesitated. "Do you mind if I ask how did you become a vampire? Become, right? I mean, you're not born that way?"

Matt froze, an avalanche of memories stabbed his undead heart. His mortality ended in this building long before she was born.

"I don't want to be rude, but…" He rose. "There's nothing more you need to know. Stay away from Brad. Stay out of the art department. Have a good life." With vamp speed, he escaped the situation before Cat could react.

The convenience of vamp agility, which almost rivaled teleportation, allowed Matt to be nothing more than red taillights in the distance by the time Cat reached the front door of her building. His supersensitive hearing caught her sudden indrawn breath immediately before he turned the corner and escaped her life forever.

As he drove, Matt considered his vow never to get involved with human females. They broke too damn easily. That was a truism he'd only needed to learn once, and much to his regret.

What were the odds, his mind raged.

What were the odds her apartment building would be that one? What were the odds the only human he'd taken an interest in for decades had led him to the site of his death?

Against his will, Matt's mind replayed her question.

How did you become a vampire?

****

Blood Emerald by Amber Anthony

SDV (Single Dom Vampire) unknowingly ISO compassionate, sincere, spontaneous SMW (Single Mortal Woman). Extra points for patience, brains, and beauty. Handsome, powerful, Rick Hiatt has managed romance and sex within the roles of Dom/sub relationships for five hundred years. What if there is something more? What if the delicious Anna Curley, shielded from the world of dark sex games, can show him?

Rick returns to the helm of his international BDSM Empire after confronting a disaster within his vampire Family. His nemesis, Veronique Moreau, could destroy the fragile veil between the Vamp/Mortal worlds, leaving vampires exposed. He meets Anna, a guileless young woman with enough savvy to see trouble coming in the form of a vampire hunter.

Their worlds collide. Swept into the dangers of preternatural conflict, Rick and Anna experience exquisite passion and heart-stopping peril. Is love enough? They could lose their lives as well as their hearts.

Blood Emerald Excerpt

Rick dressed for the night, giving up on any rest. A quick pint from whatever donor lingered at the club would sustain him. He had safety decisions to make about this damn vamp hunter that could impact the entire Los Angeles vampire Family. He only hoped he hadn't burned bridges that might be crucial to them now.

There were times when he could be too much of a smartass prick for his own good, Rick mused. It was born of being several hundred years old and perched at the top of the food chain. It didn't hurt that he was also handsome, physically fit and with vamp appeal, able to bed anyone who struck his fancy. Being called out on it? That pretty much went down like acid. Hadn't little Anna Cupcake tried to warn him less than six hours ago? And he had not listened.

Still, he wasn't entirely ready to give her a pass. Oh, yeah, she seemed all soft sweetness and light, but was that the truth? Where was his highly tuned vamp sense when he needed it? Probably floundering somewhere between his legs. What did she really want? Was she truly trying to warn him—or at least warn Matt—or was she in on it? That question burned the brightest. Was this some kind of payback? If so, Karma could be a bitch.

He walked purposefully into the membership office of the Gaoler. "Get me the personal info on that Anna girl who was Matt's groupie."

Helen, the matronly woman in charge of mortal donors, tapped a few strokes then looked up from her computer. "Anna Curley? That cute little thing that looks like a bonbon? I swear if I were her mother, she'd never have come through our door."

Rick raised a slightly aggrieved brow. In his experience, no one was that pure, and she was more cupcake than bonbon.

"She lives in Pasadena, or at least, she did last year." Helen withdrew her readers and leaned in conspiratorially. "Gossip is, she works at the Los Angeles County Museum of Art. The one across the street—an art historian or something. Probably a tour guide." She peered at Rick. "What brings her up? I was really glad when Matt cancelled her card."

"Get her on the phone. I wanna talk to her."

"You're not gonna let her back in, are you?"

"I didn't know you were in charge now, Helen." He snapped in a way he was sure betrayed his interest in the girl. "Just get me in touch with her."

Helen drew back, clearly affronted. "Yes, sir. I'll call you when I know something."

Rick sighed. Lately, he was batting three hundred in the asshole competition.

****

Brett gave him a wan smile before Rick strode down the stage-left theatre aisle, his scent-sense guiding him directly to Anna. He wound his way between set dressings, curtains and role-players, eyeing with interest the guy in the tux and red-satin-lined cape. He zeroed in on Anna at the props table.

Rick pressed up behind her and hissed, "Well, this is interesting. Does art imitate life?"

Anna whirled around, checking over both shoulders to see if anyone noticed him. Of course, they had, several female cast members all but drooled over the tall, good-looking guy in front of her. "I didn't know there was an art to what you did."

"Mind telling me what you're doing at vampire role-play?" Rick's gaze darted up to the rafters and back down. He flinched as the caped man skirted behind the scrim, leaving behind an odor of bravado and surging testosterone. Rick had much too much of that already.

Anna lowered her voice, "That would be your business because…?"

"Because I asked you. What are you doing here?" He insisted, his lips a grim line on his handsome face.

"The better question is, what are you doing here? You made it clear last night you had no interest in what I had to say." Anna was cool or at least attempting to be.

Rick rolled back and forth on the balls of his John Lobb loafers and slid his hands into his pockets, "You were drummed out of the life and look where you ended up." He glanced around the backstage with disdain, and his gaze landed back on her.

Anna bit back her anger, "No matter what you may think, my life doesn't revolve around vampires."

"All evidence to the contrary." Rick gestured smugly at the rack of costumes, the eight-foot table of props, and the prosthetic fangs. He felt all eyes were on them, privy to a lover's quarrel.

"Whatever." Anna turned back to her props and gritted out louder than before, "To retain dramatic authenticity, the audience is not allowed backstage." She looked at him coldly. "You need to leave."

"I can beat you home tonight," he snarled.

"Oh, I'm *so* scared."

Rick inhaled deeply, scenting her. "I know you are. I can smell it on you."

Anna's eyes narrowed darkly, "You still need to leave."

He grabbed her elbow, forcing a smile when he knew they were being observed. "We need to revisit last night's conversation. And Cupcake, you don't need to like me, to obey me."

"Fine. Clear my name at the door. I'll come to you."

****

Blood Emerald was named a TOP PICK in paranormal romance by Romantic Times and given a 4.5-star review. See the full review here: http://ndpbookreview.com/blood-emerald-by-amber-anthony/

Blood Dragon by Amber Anthony

Adam Lachlan, a tall drink of scrumptious masculinity, has been exiled from his dragon-shifter clan for the past two hundred years. His bad-boy charm has been harnessed to succeed as a Master Dom in the mortal world. He's spent decades isolating himself emotionally.

Willow Greer is beautiful, intelligent, and charming. Men have pursued her, but she's flown from them all. Willow has a secret burden. Adopted in infancy and having no explanation for shifting into a Pegasus at puberty, she's cloistered herself romantically. Without knowing the full truth of her nature, how can she commit to love?

When Adam's fire meets Willow's short fuse, flirtation is on! At the onset, secrets are guarded, but once their true selves are revealed, the complications begin. Can they overcome the problems of romance between different shifter species? Will they drop their emotional baggage and risk love's bondage?

Blood Dragon Excerpt

The sun struggled to show itself through the clouds and fog of the early February morning. Willow opened the door of the motorhome just in time to see an unbelievable spectacle.

What am I seeing? Massive wings carrying a... dragon? Is that a dragon? Wow!

Willow pinched her forearm and looked around.

Am I where I parked last night? Have I been transported through some vortex?

She walked boldly, if uncertainly, out to the end of the tree line.

I hope he isn't the fire-breathing type...

To her surprise, the creature seemed to be headed for a changing hut. The dragon made an elegant landing, and in front of her astonished eyes, the air around the creature shimmered as his human shape emerged. It was a form she'd fantasized about since their fortuitous meeting at the Dublin Airport. Willow held her breath as she spied on Adam from behind a tree.

He stood in the meager sunlight and rolled his shoulders, shook out his arms and crooked his neck from side to side. He looked over one shoulder, and then the other as if searching for something. Finally, he closed his eyes, paused, opened them again, and bellowed "Who's there?" He turned and looked directly at the tree hiding her. "I know you're there. Show yourself."

Willow sheepishly stepped from behind the tree's shelter. "Good morning." She crossed her arms in the morning chill and stood there in her pajamas.

"Are you following me?" Adam stood, hands on his slim hips. The pose accentuated his eight pack abs, flat belly, and highly toned obliques.

Willow caught her bottom lip between her teeth.

Leapin' lizards, you are perfection!

Of course, it didn't hurt the rays of the sun seemed to radiate from him. She was momentarily speechless.

His voice was low, deep, and commanding. "I asked you a question, I expect an answer."

"I think we have something in common." Her thumbs slid her pajama bottoms down her thighs, and as she stepped toward him, she wiggled her sweatshirt over her head. She could feel his eyes all over her, and she grinned behind the sweatshirt.

He huffed out a breath and shifted from one foot to the other. "Are you a dragon?"

Her impish smile emerged as she tossed the sweatshirt aside. "Not exactly."

****

Adam watched her extend her arms forward, the air became highly charged and her flesh began to mutate. Long, coltish arms and legs ended with horse's hooves, her pixie face elongated, and a brilliant black mane spread down her elegantly arched neck. With a flip of her black and white tail, Adam saw a dainty black and white paint Arabian mare where a woman once stood. At least he thought she was a horse until she lowered her head and whinnied as a pair of luminous, feathery, snowy wings with black tips extended from her withers. She trotted up to him and bumped him in the chest with her muzzle.

He put out an incredulous hand to touch her forelock. "Pegasus?" Her flashing black eyes, so like her human self, challenged him. "Okay."

****

The air tingled around him as he shifted and in two steps, they were off, soaring above Flight's End. Willow followed him as he glided over the Crater Lake, he made room for her to fly wing tip to wing tip with him, careful not to interfere with her flight. *Welcome to my home.* Adam inclined his head toward the settlement below and spoke telepathically.

So, you are real. It's not a hoax.

Willow arched her neck and flipped her tail, and he could not help admiring her graceful flight. He watched the human forms below them point up to her excitedly, the children, especially, jumped up and down as they pointed.

Adam projected. *I think you're a hit.*

They've never seen a Pegasus.

Willow shook her shimmering mane.

Let's give them a show!

Her speed accelerated as she launched herself into a half roll.

If you can't keep up, I'll understand.

Her black and white markings tumbled like a dancing harlequin as she slipped into a split-S maneuver. She watched over her shoulder as Adam followed, pulling sharply up before his tail slapped the water. With a whip of one wing, he splashed the water at her and laughed delightedly at her indignant snort.

I may not be as quick as you, Lolo, but can you do this?

Adam swept in a circle over the lake and projected a stream of fire, blood red as his deepest coloring.

Willow snorted again.

That's hardly a test of agility, but I will give you points for originality.

She was off again, Adam hovered in place as Willow beat her wings to fly a lazy figure eight above him.

If she's this limber in the air, I can only imagine how we'd tear up the sheets.

Willow's flight abruptly halted, and she hovered muzzle to muzzle. In the air over the crater, the mighty size of his dragon was contrasted by her petite Pegasus, yet she was undaunted by his commanding wing spread.

You know, I can hear your thoughts. And yes, I can be more flexible than you'd ever imagine.

Damn! C'mon!

Adam led her back over the crater's edge and low over the rooftops of the waking village, where school children waved to them as they headed into class. They rose over the treetops of the forest that retained their pine scent even during the winter. Adam loved their crispness. They dipped low over a sparkling, rushing river, and saw eagles grabbing their breakfast from frigid waters. Then soared up again, over a snow-dusted mountain top and buzzed the remnants of an ancient castle sitting at the mouth of the loch. Elk looked up at them as they flew back toward home.

Our flight is exhilarating. What a beautiful place this is! Why would you ever leave?

Willow exclaimed, touching her dainty hooves in a perfect landing.

Adam landed and shifted immediately. "It is beautiful when I can share it with you!"

Willow shifted and grabbed her clothes up before her, while Adam dug in his duffle for jeans. "All this flying has made me hungry! Have you eaten breakfast? Would you like to join me in my motorhome?"

I'd be a fool to admit I ate my weight in breakfast before I left.

"I'd love to share some breakfast with you."

Adam stared at her intently as she dressed, and finally stepped into his clothes. She was shivering.

Are these shivers from cold or anticipation?

He instinctively wrapped an arm around her but noticed she was barefoot. "Where are your shoes?" He slung one muscular arm under her knees and proceeded to carry the laughing woman to her motorhome.

When they got to the steps, she demanded. "Put me down. I promise you'll bang your head on the door if you don't."

Adam let her feet hit the dewy grass. "It wouldn't be the first time."

She pulled open the door and looked over her shoulder. "I'll say mind your head, anyway, this might be a tight fit for you."

Adam stood on the bottom step and poked his head into the motorhome. Looking both ways and up, he leered. "I like tight fits. It's cozy, but it has every modern convenience."

"With the equipment I saw, I'll bet everything's a tight fit."

Adam crooked a devilish grin and stepped into the cramped interior.

"I'd be happy to evaluate your equipment." He immediately bent his knees to avoid hitting the ceiling.

"We'll see." She shrugged.

****

-Blood Dragon has been given 5 Stars by Nom de Plume. For the full review follow this link: http://ndpbookreview.com/blood-dragon-by-amber-anthony/

*We hope you enjoyed reading our novella
and excerpts from The Blood Trilogy.*

Where to follow Amber Anthony:
www.AmberAnthonyWrites.com
https://www.facebook.com/WriteAmber/
GoodReads: Amber Anthony
BookBub: Amber Anthony
Twitter: @WriteAmberA

Do you enjoy Tea?
Check out our teas custom blended for
each of our books and many of our characters.
Adagio.com   Patrice Bader Blends

Books by Amber Anthony

Arise, My Darling
Becoming Gabriel

Blood Fugue
Blood Legacy

Appetite for Blood
Blood Rising
Blood Emerald
Blood Dragon

Roman's Revenge
Roman's Rules
Roman's Return

Audio through Audible
Appetite for Blood
Blood Rising
Blood Emerald